The Body at Back Beach

by

KJ Sweeney

Copyright Notice
This is a work of fiction. Names, characters, places, and incidents are either the product of the author's imagination or are used fictitiously, and any resemblance to actual persons living or dead, business establishments, events, or locales, is entirely coincidental.

The Body at Back Beach

COPYRIGHT © 2023 by Kelly Jo Sweeney

All rights reserved. No part of this book may be used or reproduced in any manner whatsoever without written permission of the author or The Wild Rose Press, Inc. except in the case of brief quotations embodied in critical articles or reviews.
Contact Information: info@thewildrosepress.com

Cover Art by *Lea Schizas*

The Wild Rose Press, Inc.
PO Box 708
Adams Basin, NY 14410-0708
Visit us at www.thewildrosepress.com

Publishing History
First Edition, 2024
Trade Paperback ISBN 978-1-5092-5487-3
Digital ISBN 978-1-5092-5488-0

Published in the United States of America

Dedication

To Mike; it seems fitting that my first book should be dedicated to you. You helped me deliver our other four babies. The labor for this one has been much longer, but much less painful.

Chapter 1

Helena couldn't say what caught her attention initially. Standing and looking up at the slip, something was not as it should be. A group of branches erupting from the earth drew her gaze, stripped of bark, and bleached white with age. But, as she'd continued to look, it had become obvious what they were.

The bones of a skeletal arm sticking out of the ground may well have been the last thing Helena expected to see while out on a walk that afternoon. But there was no denying what they were. Those long, bleached white objects were not old branches or tree roots, but finger bones. The slip in the bank had uncovered something sinister and unexpected.

Helena felt sick. Suddenly, the cold air and dark sky were overwhelming. She struggled to tamp down the fluttering, panicked feeling squeezing her chest. This was supposed to be the chance to get some fresh air. The recent storms had forced her to stay inside more, not getting out and stretching her legs. Now, finally out here for the first time in what felt like weeks, she had stumbled on something else the storms were responsible for.

The bank was little more than mud and soil, and after the recent weather, they didn't always hold up well. In more than one place, there were small slips where mud, rocks, and branches had fallen onto the track below, blocking access to vehicles and creating fresh angry gouges where the unstable ground had crumbled and fallen. The place where the bones protruded was one of the worst slips. It must have disturbed whatever had been hidden there, and now part of this body or skeleton, or whatever these strange-looking objects were, had been uncovered.

She had been so sure that walking the track around Back Beach would bring her peace and clarity. It was such a wonderful place to walk, and others felt the same. Being here alone had been a real treat and with the heavy rain they had been suffering recently, it was a welcome one. There were still heavy clouds precariously suspended in the sky, threatening to embark on another deluge. Even on wild and stormy days, the views across the harbor were stunning and instantly created relaxation and peace. Right now, that feeling was a long way off. If anything, being alone was the last thing anyone would want. If only someone could be here as well. Someone who could confirm what those strange objects were. Someone who could help decide what to do.

There was no avoiding it. Getting a closer look would surely help, even though the thought made her heart race. Trying to climb up the slip seemed to be the best option. But no, a few tentative steps forward and it soon became clear the ground wasn't safe. Even before reaching the bright orange netting barrier that had been hastily erected blocking a usually popular walking track, the ground began to move. The slip hadn't completely settled, and loose stones were already rolling away under her feet. Getting close enough to look might be possible but would run the very real risk of finding herself engulfed by a mountain of mud and earth. Rather than discovering a body, there was a very real chance of being buried in this resting place herself. No, risking getting any closer to it was simply not a good idea.

Helena reached into her pocket and pulled out her phone. Despite the wonderful feeling of isolation here on Back Beach, it was just an illusion. Civilization was only minutes away and help shouldn't take long. Surely what she had seen was nothing more than a product of an overactive imagination. Perhaps she should just leave it. If there was something there then surely someone else would notice and it would be their problem to deal with. If there really was a body up there, then there was no option but to call the police. Taking a deep but shaky breath, she dialed emergency services quickly before there was any chance to talk herself out if it.

"Police please," she said to the operator. Nibbling on the corner of her thumb while waiting for the call to be connected. Eager to pass the responsibility of the discovery to someone else. The sudden sound of a voice on the other end asking about the emergency made her jump, nerves strung right on the edge. "Hi, yes. I think there might be a body buried in the side of the hill here. The land has slipped away, and I can see what looks like fingers and an arm, well, a skeleton." Her words came out in a rush. Running fingers through her hair with agitation, she paced back and forth.

"Can you give me your location please?" the brisk voice on the other end asked.

"Oh, yes, sorry. I'm at Back Beach in Port Chalmers, on Peninsula Beach Road, around past the boat sheds." Helena gestured toward the boat sheds standing behind her, as though the person on the other end could see them through the phone line.

"And you can see a person buried. Are they injured or able to move? Is the person breathing?"

"No, oh, no. It's not a person, or at least not now it isn't. Just, well, bones." She paused, peering up at the bank where the arm seemed to have become more obvious. "It looks like a skeleton arm. I mean it might be nothing, of course, but that's what it looks like. The bank has shifted away and slid down and kind of uncovered something. It's old, I think, not recent." Helena shifted from one foot to the other, agitation mounting. The body, if it was a body, had died a long time ago. Having found it like this left her feeling nervous and on edge. Almost as though someone might be watching.

"We'll send someone out to you. Are you able to stay in your location until someone arrives?"

"Yes, of course, no problem." Helena bit back the impulse to demand they come quickly. The sooner someone else came here to face this with her, the better.

"The local constable from Port Chalmers should be with you shortly."

The call ended and she looked back up at the slip. If there was going to have to be a wait for someone to arrive, then it might be sensible to do something constructive. Perhaps try again to get a little closer to see if there weren't any mistakes about what was buried there. It soon became obvious; the ground was unstable and to move any closer would be foolish at best. Sitting and waiting for the police to arrive would be the only sensible course of action.

The Body at Back Beach

Helena looked around for somewhere to sit, as far away from the macabre discovery, while waiting. A small picnic table stood next to the entrance to the path. Even so, it was impossible to drag her eyes away from the bank. As foolish as it sounded, it was almost as though looking away might cause it to disappear and she would be just wasting everyone's time. Although, being honest, it would be much better if it was just sticks or something else completely innocuous.

The sun continued to fight its way through the cloud cover overhead but still, no one else had ventured out and about. The threat of rain had kept everyone else indoors. Why, when something like this happened and it would be really comforting to have a friendly face or two passing by, did it have to be so quiet? The noises from the distant port did not help making the track feel any less isolated. The boats moored in the small bay were creaking and groaning as they bobbed on the sea, doing little to reassure her. Every bang or other tiny noise coming from that direction was another assault on the nerves.

Helena stretched. Surely, this was a sign that exercise was not beneficial after all. She had been trying to make a real effort to keep fit and active in the last few years. Her husband, David, had always been active. As they got older, unless exercising regularly, keeping up with him when they went on tramps together became impossible. When it came to her grown-up sons, there was simply no chance of keeping up with them. She'd given up the idea of having as much energy as they had when they were toddlers and now, twenty years on, the two of them were still running rings around both of their parents.

Surely, they wouldn't be much longer. Sitting still, the cold was beginning to bite. Her jacket felt damp, even though it wasn't raining, and the fabric seemed to cling to her, chilling right through to the bone. Maybe it was being fanciful, but since she'd seen the arm, the temperature seemed to have dropped even further. Rubbing her arms didn't make much difference. Standing up and walking up and down, stamping her feet to get the feeling back might do the trick.

Despite it being only mid-afternoon, the sun had yet to make an appearance today, and the chill in the air had already started to set in. If it hadn't been so uncomfortable, Helena would have probably appreciated the view more. Although the working port was in front of her, it was hard to see much of it from this angle. Smaller surrounding islands appeared to be guarding the entrance to Dunedin and Otago beyond. In the distance, the open sea was just visible, where early settlers would have made their way through the harbor and to Port Chalmers to start a new life.

It felt as though she had been sitting there for hours before the sound of tires crunching over the gravel that made up the stone road reached her. The speed limit around here was thirty kilometres an hour and even with the prospect of a body to deal with, the police car wasn't pushing much beyond that. Helena stood in the center of the track so they wouldn't miss her and waited for it to pull up.

Only one police officer sat in the car. Helena recognized her as the constable stationed at Port Chalmers. There was a large police station building in town, but it had been left over from the days when the town itself had been busier. These days, the family flat above and cells behind were long empty, mostly being used as storage space. The police officer climbed out of the car, pulled on a hat, and walked to her.

"Constable Sarah Hanover," she said, holding out her hand. "I understand you've found a body?" Constable Hanover glanced toward the bank as she spoke, not seeming to be overly anxious to get any closer to Helena's grisly discovery.

"Hi. I'm Helena and, yes, well, an arm, possibly." Helena shook the other woman's hand and then turned to the start of the footpath leading the way. "Over here."

The policewoman followed Helena over to the orange fencing. Younger than Helena, perhaps in her early thirties, the woman exuded an aura of athleticism and strength, although that could have been a feeling created by the uniform. Sensible boots and dark blue trousers gave a welcoming impression of power and authority.

"Just there." Helena pointed to the bank where the bones were visible. "I didn't spot it at first, but I think it looks as though there might be more there, buried in the bank."

Helena and Constable Hanover stood peering up at the slip together. The policewoman took a few steps forward, but Helena reached out to grab her arm, knowing the ground wasn't stable.

"Yes, you're right, that's definitely some bones," Constable Hanover said with a slight sigh. "Sorry, don't mean to sound as though you've been a nuisance. It's absolutely the right thing to call it in. It's just it's chaos at the moment, road closures all over the place, and now a potential body to deal with."

"Sorry," Helena said with a small smile.

"Of course, it may be an old burial or even an animal. It's surprising how human-like an animal skeleton can look." Giving an almost imperceptible little shudder, Helena was sure the policewoman didn't quite believe what she said. Perhaps just an attempt to minimize the horror of what had been uncovered.

"There's no way of knowing until we get a closer look though," the constable continued. "We'll get the scene crime officers in and see what we've got." She walked back over to the police car and leaned in to talk into the radio.

Helena turned back to the bank to look at the skeletal hand. Who did it belong to and how had it ended up there? If the bank hadn't slipped away like that, the bones could have remained buried for years. Perhaps they never would have been found. Of course, there was a chance that it was just an animal. But the more she looked, the more it looked human to the untrained eye.

"I'll need to take your details, please."

Helena startled.' She hadn't noticed that Constable Hanover had returned to her side. "Your name, a brief statement of what you found, and how we can get hold of you. You should be able to go then."

Constable Hanover walked back to the small picnic table and motioned for Helena to sit down. Pulling out a pad and pen, she sat on the other side of the bench.

"Just the basics. It's getting cold, and I don't want to keep you for longer than I need to. I can get a proper statement at the police station tomorrow."

It still felt rather unreal to be talking about what had happened, how she had just stumbled across the remains. All her life she'd been a bit dismissive of the words people use to reduce the finality of death. Talking of passing or slipping off their mortal coil, but here it seemed better to avoid saying 'the body.' As she told the story of what had happened, the police officer scribbled in the notebook but said little.

Helena paused and looked up at the bank. It was impossible to keep her eyes off the arm—it just lay there, daring her to look. Constable Hanover stopped writing and followed Helena's gaze toward the bank. For a moment, neither spoke, lost in their own thoughts. Helena swallowed, took a deep breath, and continued the story.

"Once I saw the bones and realized what they were, I decided to call the police. If there had been someone else here, I could have asked what they thought about it, but, well, you see what it's like today. There's no one out and about," Helena explained.

"Did you walk to find someone to help?" Constable Hanover asked as she continued to write in the notebook, the pen flying across the page.

"No, it sounds silly, I mean, they weren't going anywhere, but I didn't like to leave the bones on their own. I don't really know why."

"Mm-hmm," the policewoman said, scribbling more in the book. "I may need a more detailed statement from you later if I can get your contact details?"

"Yes, of course. Helena Statham. I live in Sawyers Bay. Oh, and I should have a card somewhere with my phone number on it. Hang on." Rifling through her pockets, her fingers closed around her wallet. There were several small white business cards, all printed with her name and number used for clients at the university. Working as a counselor, helping students deal with the stresses and strains of life, was something that she had been doing for all her adult life. Today, for a change, she was the one who needed someone to help deal with what was going on. She handed one to Constable Hanover, who tucked it into the notebook.

"You're fine to leave. Either I will be in touch or one of the detectives to arrange to take a further statement tomorrow," Constable Hanover said. "Is your car parked far away? Will you need a lift?"

Helena couldn't shake the feeling that the policewoman was just as unnerved by the grisly discovery of the buried body as she had been, despite the cool efficiency of having to deal with the situation. Finding a skeleton surely could not be part of a normal day for her.

"Oh, no, it's just parked outside the library. It won't take me long to get there and collect it." Helena gestured vaguely with her arm toward the direction she needed to walk in.

"Great. Well, I'll let you go then. Thanks for contacting us about this."

"Thank you, bye." Helena felt suddenly eager to get away from the skeleton now that responsibility had been passed onto someone else. She set off toward the car park. This part of the road could sometimes be a little busier than the rest of the track. There were often people coming to their boat shed or workers from the port using the roadside to park on, but there still seemed to be little sign of anyone today.

Helena walked quickly, whether it was because the night had already started drawing in or the haunting event of the night, it was hard to say. The cold bit through her jacket. With hands shoved deep into her pockets and her head hung low, she walked as fast as she could. The walk back to the library took around ten minutes, which surely was faster than she'd ever managed before. Several police vans and cars drove past on their way around to the discovery site before she had reached her car. It was up to them to deal with it all now.

****

Constable Sarah Hanover stood and looked at the arm. There was no way to get closer for a better view. Soon the place would be overrun with the specialists and detectives, whose job it was to deal with bodies and suspicious deaths. Despite what she had said to Helena, she was reasonably confident this wouldn't turn out to be an animal—it looked like part of a body. This one could be ancient for all anyone knew, but until they'd established how long the body had been lying there, it would be treated as a potential murder site. Part of Sarah desperately wanted to be involved with the investigation, but the sensible side knew now wasn't the time. There was enough on her plate without having a murder investigation to worry about. Still, it was nice to be first on the scene for a change.

The first cars began to arrive, with detectives, forensic scientists, and all those highly trained people whose life's work was to investigate deaths and other violent crimes. Sarah was quite happy to hand over what she knew to them and then head back to the police station, helping them set up a temporary base. She felt at home there, in her station. Being part of the community was the part of the job she loved most of all. She was eager to get back to that side of her role and leave this to the detectives from Dunedin.

Chapter 2

Helena felt uneasy for the rest of the day. Usually, she would be the one helping other people deal with their worries and problems—being the one with problems was a completely new experience. The sight of the skeletal arm just kept running through her mind on repeat. For years she had worked at the University as part of the counseling service, but recently she had reduced hours. Funding had been cut and Helena decided it would be an ideal opportunity to step back a bit. She'd returned to full-time work when the boys had started school, but now, after over fifteen years in the same role, it felt like it was time to spend a little time doing something different. There was still plenty of paperwork to get through at home, but with less time spent in contact with the students, things should settle down soon too.

Working from home had been the plan for today, but it just wasn't holding her attention. The temptation to pick up the phone was just too great. Looking at the local paper and radio websites, skimming through Twitter feeds, and browsing through local Facebook groups was impossible to resist. Social media and gossip always seemed to pick up on news more quickly than newspapers and television news did. But she could find no mention of the body she'd discovered anywhere. It was almost enough to make her think she'd imagined it. Surely there must be someone who knew what was going on out there.

Things like that didn't happen around here. Even if they were old bones, there would be something about it somewhere. Restlessly reaching for her phone, for what must have been the thousandth time, it was just the same. Nothing. Not even a phone call from David, even though she'd called and texted him plenty of times herself.

Finally, she turned off the computer and walked into the kitchen. Rummaging through the fridge and cupboard, it was time to start sorting out the evening meal. She and David usually took turns to cook. He'd be home shortly and no doubt feeling just as hungry. It would be a good idea to get things ready for his arrival. Cooking wasn't something that she minded, but not quite the same way David enjoyed it. He would probably be quite happy to leave all the cooking to him, but as he often didn't get in until quite late, it made sense they took it in turns. On a day like today, when she was going to work, having the meal ready as he got home would be perfect.

A simple pasta dish would do for tonight. Humming as she began to chop vegetables, her mind still wouldn't settle. She pushed her fringe off her forehead with the heel of her hand, and the knife held out of the way. Helena hesitated before reaching over and turning on the radio on the kitchen worktop. Perhaps there would finally be some news, and if not, it might be a good distraction for a bit. To begin with, the program was about some political story, so she wasn't concentrating on it, but suddenly something caught her attention.

The Body at Back Beach

"...in Port Chalmers, near Dunedin," the radio announced. Helena stood still to listen after reaching over to turn up the volume, her heart rate increasing and her mouth going suddenly dry as the report continued.

"The body was uncovered in the recent bad weather. We understand that a slip had caused part of the skeleton to be exposed and it was spotted by a walker this morning. Local constable Sarah Hanover was first on the scene."

Constable Hanover's voice came over the radio, in what was obviously a pre-recorded statement. *"At this stage, we can't say who this body might be, or how long they have been in the ground. We can say this isn't a recent burial, though, and we are following several lines of inquiry currently.*

"We will be following this story and will let you know once we have more information on this discovery," said the presenter. *"And now on Checkpoint, we'll be looking at some of the other areas of the country that have been suffering from the recent bad weather."*

Helena clicked off the radio and sat at the table. The story had finally made the news, but they seemed to know even less about things than she did. It was hard to know what to expect, but hearing the report turned out to be a bit of an anti-climax. Any hopes to have learned something more once the media got involved came to nothing. It must be too early for them to know anything yet.

A few minutes later, she still sat, staring off into space, when David came through the door. In his mid-fifties, a little older than Helena, he was still a handsome man. They had been married for nearly thirty years, and it was always fun to tease him that he had aged like a fine old wine. Even so, she still found him just as attractive as ever. These days, his hair had turned a steely gray colour, rather than the dark waves of his youth. But a smile still shone in his green eyes as he greeted her. He'd lived in New Zealand since his early twenties, just before he'd met Helena, but he still retained his Northern English accent and straightforward approach to life.

"Hi. You look miles away," he said with a grin, kissing her on the cheek. "Did you hear the local excitement? Someone found a body or something, in Port."

He peeled off the light jacket he wore over the top of his cycling gear and dropped it onto the back of one of the dining chairs. He reached up to rumple his hair, which had been squashed flat by his cycle helmet. Turning toward him, Helena managed little more than to look at him blankly.

"I did. I mean, it was me who found it."

He turned to look at her, his eyebrows shooting into his hairline.

"You found it?" he asked. "Oh my God, are you okay?" He rounded the table and leaned over to give her a quick hug and a kiss.

"Yes, I sent you a text and left a message on your phone. Didn't you get it?"

"Ah, sorry, the phone's flat again." He held up the offending article with a rueful grin. Holding back a laugh, she rolled her eyes and shook her head. Modern technology and David waged a daily battle, with neither of them ever coming off the victor.

"Typical, when is it not flat?" She was accustomed

to not being able to reach him, but today it would have been nice to hear his reassuring and comforting voice. It was impossible to be really angry, though, glad he was finally there.

"Guilty, sorry. So, what happened?" He moved back around the table, pulled out a chair, and dropped into it, facing her.

She shivered slightly as she recounted the walk, clearly picturing once again the sinister discovery.

"Wow, are you all right?" He reached over to grab her hand "Pretty exciting, though. What did they say?"

"I'm not sure I'd call it exciting. It was a bit creepy, really. They didn't say a lot. Sarah something, the young female constable from Port, came out for it. She was on the radio earlier. Just said they were looking into it. I think I've got to give another statement tomorrow." She shrugged her shoulders, dealing with the police and taking part in murder inquiries wasn't something she had any experience of. "It was a bit strange, to be honest, but I'm okay, I didn't get close to it or anything and the police dealt with it all." She gave a slightly forced smile but already she began to feel more like her usual self.

"Pretty eventful day for you then?" David said. He stood up from the table and pulled a bottle of wine out from the rack on the side. He held it up in silent question and Helena nodded, continuing to talk as he poured them both a glass.

"Not really. I mean, I've not been able to stop thinking about it, but I didn't do anything. I didn't know it was a whole body until I heard it on the news just now. All I saw were a few bones that may or may not have been a hand." Shivering again, she took a sip of the wine. "I hope I'm not going to have nightmares about it."

David reached over and squeezed her arm. "It's not particularly nice but try not to think about it too much. It might have been there for years and be nothing sinister at all."

Helena gave him a slight smile. "I know you're right. It's just playing on my mind at the moment." Standing, she walked over to the hob where all the ingredients for the evening meal were ready. "Dinner will be about fifteen minutes. It's nearly ready."

"Great," David said, stretching with an exaggerated groan. "I'll go for a quick shower and change out of these clothes before we eat then."

Helena found herself slipping into quiet moments for the rest of the evening. What had happened was never too far from her thoughts. More than once she spotted David glancing at her with concern, but he seemed to think that, for the time being at least, she wasn't ready to keep talking about it. He knew her well.

It wasn't until they were in bed that night that she found herself wanting to talk about it more. After reading the same sentence over again for what must have been at least the tenth time and still not having a clue what it said, she put the book down with a sigh.

"Who do you think it is?" she asked, looking over toward David.

"Who do I think who is?" David asked, though he hadn't looked up from his book.

"The body, the one I found earlier? I can't stop thinking about it. Who is it and how long has the body been there?"

"I'm sure the police will find out." David set the

book on the table and looked at Helena. "I know you feel involved, like you're part of it because you found the body, but you mustn't go getting in the way and trying to solve whatever it is yourself. This isn't one of your murder mystery books. The police are more than capable of sorting it out." David raised a single eyebrow, emphasizing his point.

"Oh, yes, I know that. I was just thinking about it." She hoped she sounded more convincing than she felt.

"Hmm…" He was watching her closely with a slight smile playing around his lips.

"No, really, I know. I just can't help thinking about it." She lifted her reading glasses off and rubbed her eyes, placing them on the bedside table beside her, along with the now-closed book.

"No, I suppose not. I just don't want you getting caught up in something that could be dangerous. The body might have been there for ages, or it might not. There's every chance there are people who don't want someone nosing around in what's happened. It should be left to the police." He continued looking at her with a concerned frown on his face.

"I know, I know you're right." She kept nodding.

He looked at her intently. They'd been married for so long that she knew he could almost see what she was thinking, even if she didn't say anything.

She sighed. "You are right. I just can't help thinking about it at the moment. In a few days, I'll probably have forgotten all about it."

"Hmm," he said again, picking up his book but continuing to watch her.

"Anyway, I'm tired and I can't seem to concentrate on reading. I think I'll try to get to sleep." She rolled toward him and kissed him. "Night."

"Goodnight, I'll be turning my light off in a minute or two, so it shouldn't disturb you for long."

Helena rolled away from him and curled up to go to sleep. David picked up his book once more and began to read, but he couldn't help glancing over at his wife, a worried crease between his eyes.

Chapter 3

There was a brief mention of the discovery of the body on the radio and the morning breakfast news on television, but no more details than there had been the previous evening. The morning paper had nothing more than a brief paragraph about the body being found, although being local news, no doubt they would stretch it to something much bigger by the following day. The police had managed to keep the story quiet just long enough to make it too late for it to become major news yet. It wasn't to last though. Before she'd even made herself a bit of breakfast, or a cup of tea, the telephone rang.

"Hello?"

"Good morning. I'd like to speak to Helen Statham, please?"

"Helena." The caller probably just wanted her to change her electric company, or something similar, but they could at least get the right name.

"Sorry?" the confused caller asked.

"Helena, my name is Helena. How can I help you?" Helena moved around the kitchen, starting to make herself a coffee and something to eat, only half-listening to the person on the phone.

"Ah, yes, sorry, it's quite early. Haven't had enough coffee yet." The voice gave a forced laugh and then paused. "My name is Steve and I'm a journalist with the Otago Daily Times. I understand you were involved in the discovery of the body in Port Chalmers yesterday? I wanted to ask you a few questions?"

So here it was, the start of the journalists and news media wanting to know what had happened yesterday. Getting Helena to give her side of the story. It was to be expected, but somehow it was still a surprise.

"Well, yes, I suppose so." Helena leaned on the kitchen counter, sipping the coffee she'd just poured.

"Okay, can you just run me through what happened yesterday? You were walking around Back Beach in Port Chalmers?" A rustling noise came from the other end of the line.

"Yes, I'd finally got out of the house for a bit, it had stopped raining—you know how bad it's been lately. Anyway, I decided to go for a walk around Back Beach. Because of the weather, there were quite a few slips as I went around. One had covered the footpath, and as I looked at the slip, I saw it." Helena paused. How much was safe to say? The police hadn't mentioned not talking to the media, but perhaps it would have been a good idea to ask them about that.

"The body?" he asked.

"Yes, well, I didn't know it was a body. At first, I wasn't really sure what I could see. But the more I looked at it, the more it looked like some bones or something."

"Just bones? Could you tell they were human?"

"I wasn't sure, to be honest." Helena paused, remembering yesterday. "There wasn't much to see, just a few bones that looked as though they might be part of a hand."

"And what about the rest of the body? I understand

a whole body has been found?" Helena could hear more rustling and couldn't help imagining him making notes on the other end of the line.

"I don't know, I couldn't see much. The bones were sticking out of the ground. Where the slip was, I think as the land slipped, it uncovered something buried there. But not the whole lot."

"So, when you realized what you were looking at, you called the police?"

"Yes. They came and then I left. That's all I know."

"Okay, great. I think it will do for now. I'll be back in touch if we need some more info. Thanks, bye." With that, he hung up. Helena couldn't help but feel he hadn't been that interested in anything she'd been saying, just ticking a box that he'd spoken to the person who'd found the body. He didn't seem to be paying much attention to her. It was hardly surprising. The real story of the body would probably come from other places—who the person had been in life, and how they ended up there.

"Bye," Helena said, putting the phone down, even though he had already gone.

So, a corpse had been found. But whose body? How long had they been buried there? What had happened to them? It didn't seem the newspaper had learned much from her and she certainly hadn't learned anything more from them. Not that Helena stopped thinking about it. She had to go and find out more about the body she'd discovered. Perhaps there was some way to even help solve the mystery. Being an amateur detective hadn't been something that had ever been part of Helena's plan, but now it seemed irresistible. Even without some of the other necessary skills of investigation, Helena knew people, which would surely be helpful. Years of working as a councilor at the university meant exposure to all kinds of different people. Maybe the experience would come in useful?

Getting out of the house would also mean avoiding any more phone calls like the one she'd just received, or even worse, journalists turning up on the doorstep. Not that it was likely to happen here, but she'd seen people being hounded by the press on television before. She had no desire to become the latest local sensation. Grabbing jacket and keys, Helena headed for the door.

****

For the time of year, Port Chalmers was busy. In the summer, the small town was often bustling due to the large cruise ships berthing there every few days and the tourists coming to visit. During the winter months, things were quieter. Especially on dull overcast days like today. But of course, today wasn't a normal day. There were more cars than usual and far more people moving around. As news of the discovery spread, it brought more people into the town. There were television crews, reporters, and ordinary members of the public who had come just to try and find out the most recent news, to get to the bottom of what had happened. The normally quiet police station now had extra police officers going in and out of the front door.

Helena wasn't sure about speaking to any more journalists, especially not until there was a chance to speak to the police about what she should or shouldn't say. Reporters would no doubt try to build a story out of her tiny involvement.

She wasn't sure where the best place to start was. It

wasn't as though walking into the police station and starting to ask questions was realistic, demanding they reveal everything they had discovered so far. While it might feel as though she was involved in the mystery, having made the initial discovery, the chances were they wouldn't see it quite that way.

This was a small community and there were plenty of other ways to find out what was happening. By speaking to the locals, Helena knew that she could find out far more, possibly even more than the police had discovered. There were certain advantages to being part of a close-knit town like this. The library would be a good place to go for information and not just what could be found in books. Some of the shops and cafes were also great places to pick up gossip and stories. Helena decided spending the morning working around the various places in the small town might be the best way to go.

She knew from experience sharing a bit of your own knowledge or gossip often was the best way to find out what you wanted to know. People couldn't resist filling in the blanks and letting you know they were just as much in the know as you were, perhaps even more so—such is human nature. So, Helena decided to use the advantage of being first on the scene to its full potential.

After parking on George Street, she looked around and decided where the gossip would be. Even before speaking to anyone, it was almost as though she could hear the town talking. A liveliness and buzz seemed to hang in the air, almost as though people could actually be heard talking about what had happened behind closed doors and in the shops along the main road. The questions seemed to float around on the street.

"Did you hear about the body?"

"All these police everywhere, do you think it's murder?"

"I wonder who it is?"

"How long have they been there?"

"Have you heard?"

"Did you hear?"

Helena couldn't be sure if her imagination had got the best of her, driven by her insatiable curiosity. The air seemed different today, a feeling something was happening and had woken up the town from its winter hibernation.

Helena walked through the door of the chemist. It also served as the local post shop and, as a result of visiting at least a couple of times a month, wasn't out of the ordinary. If it wasn't to collect a parcel or send something herself, then its other function was handy for sticking plasters, painkillers, and slightly fancier hair products and cosmetics than the local supermarkets stocked. She was a regular enough customer to be on small talk and greeting acquaintances with the staff, if not quite on first-name terms.

Helena walked through the front door, heading to the long desk at the rear of the shop that served as checkout, a place for consultation with the pharmacist and post office counter.

"Have you heard about this body they've found?" the lady serving asked her before she'd even fully reached her. Helena knew her name was Janet. "It's all anyone has been talking about this morning."

"Yes." Helena braced herself, in readiness for taking the role as the center of the town grapevine.

"Actually, I found it."

"Noooooo," Janet said, whether, from surprise or the pleasure of having a new source of information to mine, Helena wasn't sure. Possibly both. "Yesterday?"

"Yes, when I went for a walk around Back Beach." Helena realized more information would have to be shared if she wanted to learn anything herself. "I didn't know what I saw at first, but I could see something wasn't right. I thought it might be a bit of bone or something, so I called the police."

"How frightening. You must have been terrified, finding a dead body like that. It must have been awful for you," Janet said, leaning on the counter, all thoughts of enquiring what Helena might actually have come into the shop for this morning clean out of mind. Janet gazed at Helena with rapt attention, thrilled to find herself so close to the drama.

"Well, at the time, I wasn't entirely sure what I'd found. Then, by the time the police arrived, it all seemed a bit unreal."' Helena paused for a moment. Of course, she'd known the body must have belonged to someone, to have been someone once upon a time. For some reason, though, the idea someone had died hadn't been fully absorbed until that very moment. This wasn't an abstract puzzle to solve. This was someone's life, or at least it had been, once upon a time.

"Sorry," Helena began again, shaking her head to clear the sudden disquiet settling over her. "It still seems very unreal."

Janet nodded sympathetically. "And could you see much of them, whoever it was?"

"No," Helena admitted, shaking her head.

"It could have been there for years, of course, some

ancient burial." Janet paused. "They're looking at all the houses above the slip, though. Mary Newsom, do you know her, from Magnetic Street?"

Helena indicated that it wasn't someone she knew, but it didn't matter to Janet, she just wanted to have her part in retelling the story.

"Well, she told me the police have cordoned off all the gardens on the side of Magnetic Street and Island Terrace that back onto the slip and where the body was found. She's on the other side of the street, but one of her neighbors had been telling her. The police have been there all yesterday evening and this morning, hunting for something or other."

"They think the body came from one of the gardens?" Helena frowned and tried to remember where Magnetic Street was and where it fit into the bank above Back Beach. Could the body have come from the garden of one of those houses? It hadn't been possible to see if any of the houses from the properties above had land slip down, but her attention hadn't been on that area—the bones had taken all of her focus.

"It looks like it. There were a few that lost a bit of land in the latest slip. I'm not sure if they know which house it came from, though. If it's slipped from a garden, it can't be old though?"

"I wouldn't have thought so, no. Unless the land hadn't been disturbed when the houses were built." Helena pondered for a moment. "I can't picture which house would have been above where I was standing."

"No, and the land around there has moved so much in all of this rain, it could be any of them," Janet said, falling quiet as though picturing the street.

Glancing at her watch, Helena said, "I'd better be

getting on. you'll have to let me know if you hear anything else?"

"See you later," Janet replied.

Helena left the shop. In the excitement of sharing details of the discovery, neither she nor Janet had noticed she hadn't bought anything from the shop or given any reason for calling in. The interest in the discovery yesterday seemed to be affecting the whole town, not just her.

The main street had a selection of shops. Some, like the pharmacy, were used mostly by locals. Others, like the various gift shops and those selling knick-knacks, jewelry, and other non-essentials were frequented by the large numbers of tourists who flocked to the town. At this time of the year, with very little in the way of tourist customers around, most of these shops were closed or opening just at the weekend. Helena made her way down the street and into the cafe at the end.

It was a cozy little place with large windows that looked out on the main street and down to the entrance to the port itself. The perfect place to sit and watch the world go by. Helena often came in once or twice a week for a flat white on days when working from home. It was always popular; it would be unusual to find it without at least one or two customers. Today, it seemed more people than usual were there—no doubt eager to hear more about what had been discovered around Back Beach.

"Well, I don't know of anyone who's gone missing recently."

Helena recognized the woman who spoke, having seen her around and about the town from time to time.

Her name was one that she remembered hearing but had never spoken to her before. Walking up to the counter, the two women standing there noticed her, turned, and smiled, drawing her into their conversation.

"You've heard about this body they found?" the second woman asked Helena.

"Yes, round by Back Beach?" Helena didn't feel the need to elaborate on the role in the drama she'd already played. It might also be a good idea to avoid identifying herself with people she didn't recognize. Giving an impromptu interview to a journalist didn't seem to be a good plan.

"The police were in here earlier, weren't they," said the first woman, turning to the lady behind the counter, who had just come out of the kitchen at the back to serve, prompting her to share the information. Helena had a smiling acquaintance with the woman having been served by her several times before. Maybe in her mid-forties, Helena would have guessed, with long blonde hair and a bubbly personality—possibly to make up for being quite short, barely able to see over the high counter.

"Yes, they've been in and out all day. There's a lot of them here at the moment, looking at the crime scene and all of that kind of thing. I think we've had them all in here at some point for coffee or something to eat," she replied. To Helena, it sounded as though the story had been told quite a few times already, possibly to everyone who had visited the cafe so far. Like Janet at the pharmacy, savoring her role in the drama, no matter how small.

"I imagine you've been quite busy," Helena said. "Did they tell you anything about it?"

"Me? No," she replied with a smile. Helena knew the woman would have loved to have been confided in by those investigating, feeding all kinds of information she could share with her customers, 'strictly in confidence' of course. "All hush-hush police business."

"But you heard them talking about it?" prompted the second woman.

"Well, yes, two of them were talking about some fabric found with the body." Giving up the knowledge as though almost reluctant to share it, but it wasn't entirely convincing, the eager gleam in her eyes giving things away.

"And they were talking about people going missing thirty years ago, weren't they?" interrupted the first woman, unable to contain excitement over the local adventure.

"One of them in here said he was looking back at disappearances over the last thirty years. Of course, I said I couldn't think of anyone, but it might not be someone from around here. I think we'd all know about someone who was missing for that long."

The two women nodded sagely at this, and Helena found herself joining in. She hadn't lived in the area thirty years ago, so there was no chance she'd have even the first idea of who the body could be. Were there any high-profile missing person cases from back then? It wasn't the kind of thing you forgot about. Surely if someone had vanished, even thirty years ago, it would have been on the national news? New Zealand was a small country, and it would be unusual for a missing person story to go unnoticed.

"What can I get you then?" Rebecca, the lady behind the counter, asked Helena, remembering what they were all there for. Helena's mind had been wandering, but this dragged her back to the present. It was surprising just how easy it was to get more information about the burial.

Helena ordered the usual flat white, making her way to one of the large windows at the front of the building. A wooden shelf on the windowsill was used as a table. There were only a few other tables in the whole place and with the extra people around, there wasn't any room in the rest of the cafe. It didn't really matter, though, as this gave a great view of the street outside. Helena sat on one of the small stools while waiting for the coffee. Sitting and watching the world go by while gathering her thoughts and deciding what to do and where to go next seemed a great idea.

The day was overcast, and the threat of yet more rain still hung in the air. She watched the container trucks rumbling down the road to the entrance to the port. There were also log trucks, but rather than heading straight into the port, they followed the road around toward Back Beach. Today, they weren't the only traffic heading that way. Police cars, vans and vehicles, which no doubt belonged to media and other interested parties, made their way down the road or came back from that direction every so often.

Port Chalmers was busier than Helena had ever seen it at this time of year. She turned back toward the counter as the coffee arrived. The two women hadn't moved from their previous position and were still standing discussing the case. They were talking to everyone coming into the cafe, no doubt keen to share what they knew and hoping someone would have some more information to add to their story. Helena couldn't help but feel relieved not to have shared her role in finding the body. They would no doubt have kept her talking for hours, extracting every little detail before becoming the subject of their conversation, long after leaving.

Just as she was finishing her coffee, the door to the cafe opened and Constable Hanover walked in. She spotted Helena and smiled.

"Hi. Well, you've caused quite the stir with your adventure yesterday," Constable Hanover said with a grin.

"Oh, ha ha, yes," Helena replied, with a glance at the counter, hoping that no one had overheard them. The two women were watching closely and listening to the exchange, so there was little chance her role would remain hidden for long.

"I'm going to need to just get a few more details from you later and to get a formal statement. Do you mind popping into the station?" Sarah asked.

"Yes, no worries. When do you want me?"

Constable Hanover glanced at her watch. "Sometime this afternoon? Around two, maybe?"

"Yes, that's fine. I'll see you then," Helena replied in a hurry, not wanting to be rumbled as a potential major player in this local drama before getting away. Gulping back the rest of the coffee, she gathered her things and left the cafe before being pumped for more information by the two women at the counter. She'd leave that particular pleasure to the policewoman, who could at least use her job and position as the perfect excuse for not telling them anything.

****

Helena pulled her raincoat tighter around herself.

Since she'd entered the cafe, the weather had taken a turn for the worse. Dark clouds were gathering overhead, and the wind had increased in strength. The air smelled damp and it appeared it was likely to start raining at any moment. Helena had only one more place to visit before returning home and digesting what she'd learned. She'd have to come back out to visit the police station later, but she had time to go to the library and then pop home for some lunch first. Anything to get out of this dismal weather.

The library was in a rather grand-looking stone building. Like much of the main street in Port Chalmers, it had been built at a time when the town was much busier. The lower floor had once served as the local fire station. Its grand facade fitted in more with the importance the town once had, rather than the sleepy life it led now. The building sat proudly on a corner with the main entrance facing the port. A triangular building, to fit between two roads; one which wove around to Back Beach and the other angling sharply upward to the higher streets in the town. On the other corner sat another substantial building which had once been a bank, but now sat empty and neglected. On the opposite side of the road were the cafe she had just been in and a small garden area. All four corners pointed down toward the entrance to the port itself, which in many ways continued to be the entire reason for the town's existence.

The library building was multi-purpose. It housed the library on the ground floor and the town hall on the level above. Helena loved to visit the library. It wasn't as big, or old as some she'd visited in the world, but it was a friendly space and there was always the enjoyment of being somewhere mostly populated with books.

It was fairly quiet compared to the rest of town. There were a couple of people sitting behind computers quietly tapping away. In the children's section, two small children were playing with the jigsaws and building blocks while their mother took a discrete snooze on the sofa. Helena smiled to herself, remembering those days all too clearly, when the chance of a five-minute rest felt like pure indulgence. Being a regular in the library, Helena knew the librarians fairly well. Walking over to the counter, she smiled at the lady who stood there, entering something onto the computer. The librarian, Greta, was in her midfifties and with a bright green dress and flaming red hair, not really someone who filled the stereotype of a mousy librarian. With modern technology taking much more of a role these days, Helena had noticed on previous visits that Greta was at home helping children on computers and with iPads as she was amongst the books. She had a knack for remembering everyone's name and what they liked to read, and helped the library feel like a sunny escape on a dull day like this.

"Hi, Greta, how are you? I just thought I'd pop in and see if my book had arrived," Helena said, smiling.

"Hello, Helena. Dreadful weather, isn't it? I'll just have a look for you."

Greta tapped away on the computer in front of her. Helena was fairly sure the book she had ordered wouldn't have arrived yet. Still, she'd needed some reason to come into the library. Silly, really. She often came in and browsed among the shelves and stopped for a chat with the librarians, but today felt different.

"No, it doesn't look as though it's been returned yet. I'll keep an eye out for it and give you a call when it arrives," Greta said, looking up from the screen. "I suppose you've heard the big news?"

"The body found round on Back Beach? Yes." Again, Helena felt reluctant to bring her role in the drama to everyone's attention.

"Yes, of course, I don't know much about it, to be honest," Greta said. "But Bill Harding was in here earlier and, well, you know what he's like?"

"Not really, no. Bill Harding? I don't think I know him." Helena frowned, trying to place the name.

"Oh, he lives up on Island Terrace above where they found it, or nearby at least. I think he'd been watching comings and goings all day; he does like to be the center of everything. I thought everyone knew Bill. He used to see himself as the unofficial mayor at one time. He ran the scouts, was president of the Tennis club, and did all of that charity work. He's not so prominent now, of course, not since all of the trouble when he lost his wife, but he still looks after the Pioneer Hall."

"No, I don't think I've come across him before.'" Helena had lived locally for around twenty years since moving here with Dave when their sons were small, but she hadn't been particularly involved in the local community.

"It might be a bit before your time, actually. You weren't here back then. Oh, how long ago now, it must be thirty years. Well, time does fly, doesn't it? I wouldn't have thought it was that long ago," Greta said, almost as though thinking out loud.

Helena listened intently. This wasn't directly

related to the body of course, but someone who had been around and very prominent thirty years ago might be worth talking to. If the body did date from around then, he might know something, or remember someone who had gone missing around then.

"No, we moved here just after Adam was born, and he turns twenty-four next month," Helena said.

"Twenty-four? It only seems five minutes ago you were both coming to the toddler story time," Greta said.

Helena smiled. She loved both of her sons dearly and would usually chat about them at any available opportunity. Especially now they were both grown up and moved away from home. But right now, she didn't want to be dragged away from finding out more about this mysterious body, so resisted the temptation to continue talking about her boys.

"I know, goes so fast. No, I don't think I'd know this Bill. As you say, must be a bit before my time."

"Well, he's still around, but his heart just wasn't in it anymore after his wife died. That and the situation with the girl. I can't remember her name now, pretty young thing, but, well, always a bit of trouble there. He should have known better at his age, but once his wife had died, I think he got a bit obsessed with her. She was far too young for him and had all these other boyfriends. She didn't stick around, though, and left him alone and depressed," Greta said.

"That's a bit sad, poor man." Helena shook her head. Losing your partner would be hard, and 'imagined many people had found themselves taken advantage of when alone and vulnerable.

"Yes, but he'd been terribly judgemental with others. People thought he'd got too big for his boots and had it coming. He'd been quite well thought of in the church, involved in all sorts up there. A few of them told him what they thought of him, making a fool of himself and ought to leave well enough alone. There were a few big bust-ups, and he left the church, I'm not sure what about, to be honest. He just kind of dropped out of view after that. He's still around though, runs a few events at the hall, but nothing like he used to."

Helena thought this Bill Harding might be quite useful to talk to. If he had been prominent in the community around the time this body was buried, he might know something interesting that happened around then or have an idea about who it might be. How easy would it be to get to talk to him?

Chapter 4

Helena stood outside the police station for a moment before going in. There was no reason to be fearful about going to see the police. She'd never been in trouble. The closest brush with the law had been a speeding ticket when in her twenties. Even so, it felt a little nerve-wracking about going to talk to them. Taking a deep breath, she walked up the two steps to the front door.

The police station in Port Chalmers was an impressive building, for the size of the local population at least. It looked as though it should house at least five or six policemen per shift each day, but these days there was only the one regularly stationed there. The town had once been a very busy port, bringing people and goods into the country. In the early days, it had been the gateway to Otago, the place where new settlers arrived from all over the world, but particularly Scotland, to start a new life in New Zealand. The promise of gold in central Otago had attracted fortune hunters from all over, keen to take their chances on striking it rich. These days, the port itself was still fairly busy; log trucks, container ships, and during the summer months, cruise ships came in and out. A large container storage area and piles and piles of pine logs sat at the port, ready to be shipped overseas. The activity here added to the noise and bustle of the town, bringing workers to the area and trucks to drop off and collect the goods. Apart from the seasonal visitors, no passengers were arriving regularly, and there was no longer any need for a large police presence in the town. Instead, the one lone constable had to deal with most of the minor issues on their own, calling in backup from town on the odd occasion it was needed.

The policewoman usually ran the place herself. Helena had never been inside the police station before and found herself curiously looking around. There was a small counter that made up the front desk, and a black security grill that usually separated the public from the officers was raised. Helena could hear people moving around in the building. Constable Hanover stood at the desk working on some paperwork, along with another uniformed officer talking on the telephone.

Presumably, the police had needed to set up some sort of incident room or base in Port Chalmers close to the incident. The large police station would be the obvious place for it. There was plenty of space waiting for use and it made a change for the building to be properly utilised. Constable Hanover looked up and smiled as she saw Helena walk in.

"Thanks for coming in. This shouldn't take too long. Come through," she said. "I'm just taking Mrs Statham's statement. Greg, are you okay to hold the fort here?"

The other police officer nodded and raised his eyebrows in acknowledgement, while continuing to listen to someone on the other end of the telephone. Sarah lifted the counter and ushered Helena through to a tiny room at the back of the police station. The room Helena found herself in was a small kitchen area with a kettle and microwave, obviously used as a break room or kitchen area. It didn't seem anything like the police offices or interview rooms Helena had seen on television before.

"I hope I'm not too late, Constable Hanover," Helena said, noticing the clock on the wall showing the time as almost five in the evening.

"Not at all and please call me Sarah. We try to keep things a bit more informal, this being a local station," she said with a reassuring smile. Nodding toward the clock Helena had spotted, she said, "That thing has never been right. I think it's closer to four."

Helena smiled at the policewoman's reassuring tone. Here, in the station, she seemed much more confident and relaxed than yesterday at Back Beach. It was hardly surprising.

"Sorry about this," Sarah said, gesturing around. "There isn't anywhere else free at the moment, and at least we won't be disturbed in here. I've got a few things to go over in your statement." Sarah dropped her folder down onto a small round table. She gestured to the chair on the other side for Helena to sit on.

"Can I get you a coffee or tea or something?" Sarah asked.

"No thanks, I'm fine."

Sarah sat in the other seat, opened up the folder, and brought out some papers. Flicking through the sheets for a moment, she found the pages she needed and clicked the end of her pen, looking toward Helena with a reassuring smile.

"We'll just go through what happened. If you could give me as much detail as possible that would be great. So, you were walking around Back Beach yesterday when you spotted the body?"

"Yes, I walk around there frequently. But with all the rain, I haven't had a chance, so I was quite glad to get out." Helena hoped her answer satisfied Sarah. This was the first time she had ever given a statement to the police about anything, but she was eager to help. There was something almost exciting about being involved in some way in the investigation—if you forgot about the body that had been found, but surely there was nothing she knew that would be useful to the police?

"Have you seen anything unusual around there before?" Sarah said, glancing up from her notes.

"No, not that I can think of." Helena paused for a second, casting her mind back to previous walks in the area. "Actually, I don't usually go anywhere near the path or the bank. It was only when I saw there had been a bit of a slip I went for a closer look. I usually just walk around on the flat road area."

Thinking about it now, it was almost unbelievable she had seen anything at all. How many times had she walked along there and not paid the slightest bit of attention to the bank or the path that wound its way to the streets above? Yes, she'd been looking at the damage from the recent bad weather, but even that didn't fully explain it. She couldn't remember paying such close attention to any of the other slips on the route. It would have been fanciful to think she had somehow been destined to find it. That the bones were waiting for Helena to come along and spot them. Even so, a chill ran up her spine at the thought. Shaking herself slightly, she tried to focus on what Sarah said to her. The questions seemed to be a little more than going over what she had already explained yesterday. It still didn't feel real, but the more she spoke about it, the clearer the picture appeared in her mind.

"Did you see anyone else out on your walk?" Sarah asked. "Dog walkers or joggers, someone like that?"

Helena shook her head. "No, not while I was there, anyway. I didn't see anyone, which is a bit unusual, but the weather has been so bad, hasn't it? I think everyone else just stayed warm at home."

Sarah nodded, scribbling more down as Helena spoke. "How long from spotting the body to calling the emergency services do you think?"

"I'm not sure, to be honest. As I said, I didn't know what I was looking at to start with. When I decided it was a body, I think I called more or less straight away. It's hard to say, though. I wasn't paying much attention to the time. Probably about half an hour into my walk, maybe a bit more." Helena paused, trying to see if she could remember more details.

She wondered why all the questions about other people. Had someone tampered with the bones, gone up, and disturbed them or something?

"I can imagine. It's not what you expect to come across every day, especially here in Port, is it?" Sarah said with a little laugh.

"No, it really isn't," Helena said, with a small smile. "You don't think someone else was there before me and moved them or something?"

Sarah tapped her pad for a second before looking at Helena again. As though choosing her words carefully. "We need to be sure the bones were uncovered where you found them."

Helena frowned, trying to understand her meaning. "You mean you think someone might have put them there recently?"

"We don't know, but it's something we have to look into. There's no doubt these bones are not recent, but who is to say if they have been there the whole time? Our forensic team will be able to answer some questions. If there's a chance it's a recent concealment, then the sooner we know who was there, the better."

Helena nodded. "I see. Well, as I said, I saw no one."

Sarah paused and looked down at her notes. "Was the slip active while you were there? Was there any movement or had it stopped? Could you tell?"

"No, I didn't notice any movement. It all seemed very still, to be honest. I didn't want to go too close, as it didn't look very stable. But I didn't see it move at all while I was there until I tried to get a closer look. It was only the loose stuff closer to me that moved, not where the actual bones were."

"So, the body didn't fall at all or become more exposed while you were there? It looked more or less the same as when the police arrived?"

"Yes, I didn't want to go any closer and disturb anything, but it certainly wasn't shifting from where I first saw it." Helena nodded.

As Sarah jotted down more notes, Helena relaxed a little and looked around the room. It wasn't what she had expected a police station to look like. Of course, this police station didn't get used much and it was probably very different to the big station in town. The muffled sound of voices and people moving around drifted in from a nearby room. Not something the station usually saw these days.

"And you don't know what time you started your

walk?" Sarah asked.

"Not exactly. It would have been somewhere around nine, nine-thirty, I think. I left home just after nine, I think." Helena shook her head, trying to be more accurate.

"Which way did you head on your walk?"

"I walked up George Street after parking behind the dairy, toward Albertson Ave. I walked past the side of the school and then along Muscle Bay. I walked up and around to Back Beach that way."

Helena usually went on the same route when on a walk around Back Beach. So used to going that way she didn't pay much attention to how long each stage took her. She'd never considered at the start of this walk she might need to recount details to the police or remember where and when she had been at various points. It had seemed just like another normal day. Even now, the whole thing seemed surreal, and she struggled to believe it had happened.

"Fantastic, thanks so much. I don't know if these questions will tell the detectives anything, but we have to make sure we've got all the information down." Sarah slid the sheet she had been writing on toward Helena. "If you could just read through it and then sign to say it's a true statement of what happened yesterday and when you found the remains."

Helena quickly read through the statement and then nodded, signed it, and handed it back to Sarah. With a smile, Sarah stacked up the papers and pad she had spread around the table, bringing the interview to an end.

"How are you feeling about it now? Has it affected you much?" Sarah asked, looking at Helena with concern.

"Not really. I've spoken to my husband about it, but it just doesn't seem real." Helena shrugged her shoulders. "I'm not sure how I'm supposed to be feeling."

"You might find it is something that affects you later on. When you've had time to properly absorb it all. We've got a number you can call if you need to talk to someone." Sarah hunted through the folder in front of her and pulled out a small business card and a pamphlet. "This is a support line. It's usually for people who've been involved in a violent crime or death, but they work with witnesses and family members too. I've got a fact sheet for you too, some help with crisis and trauma."

"Thanks. I'm okay at the minute, but I know these things can be delayed. It seems strange being on the other side for a change."

Sarah glanced down at her notes. "Of course. I forgot you work in a counseling service. Well, you know where to get help, but this might be a bit more specific for what you're going through. They're used to dealing with crime and its effects on people."

"Yes, thanks." Helena folded up the papers and put them into her shoulder bag. Taking a deep breath, she wondered if she should broach this. "I don't suppose you can tell me anything about the body? Have you found out how long it's been buried or who it is?"

"I can't go into much detail, as it's an active investigation, but there's going to be an appeal on the news later and I can tell you what we're going to be releasing to the public then. We're looking at missing people from around thirty years ago. We think it was a woman, but we don't know the exact age—somewhere between around fifteen and twenty-five years old. It looks as though she has been in the ground for about that long."

"Thirty years isn't long. I suppose someone might know something." Helena nodded, taking in all she had just been told. Somehow, hearing it was the body of a young woman she'd found made it seem more real. She couldn't help but wonder who the unfortunate woman was.

"Yes, we're hoping someone will come forth and give us more information. Please, do get back in touch if you remember anything else—even the smallest thing might be important."

Helena stood up. "I will do, but I don't think there was anything else, though, nothing I can think of, anyway." She frowned for a second and then gave Sarah a small smile.

****

Helena sat in the car, ready to drive home. Thirty years sounded like a long time ago. Lots of people would have moved out of the area or might have died in that time frame. But it was within many people's living memories, perhaps not clearly, but surely something big like a young woman going missing would be the kind of thing people would remember. Plenty of locals had lived here for the last thirty years and would have been here when the body had been buried. Someone must know who she was, even if they didn't know what happened. Of course, there was always a chance someone knew more than that. The poor woman hadn't buried herself. There must be someone, somewhere, who had been carrying that particular secret for the last thirty years. Still, no doubt the police would find out more soon. It wasn't something she needed to involve herself in. The sooner she forgot about her little adventure and got on with her life, the better, before she started to drive herself mad wondering and trying to find out more.

Chapter 5

Sarah pulled out the band holding her neat ponytail and raked her fingers through her hair. She was tired and beyond ready to finish for the day. She didn't need to stay much later at the police station this evening, but it didn't feel right to leave it just yet. Usually, five was home time, leaving the overnight policing of the area to the bigger police station in Dunedin. If something big happened, then she would be called back in, but that was unusual, and it was rare to work anything other than office hours on most days. Sarah loved her job, manning the small, local station in Port Chalmers. It was rare to have much trouble to deal with. There was, however, just enough excitement to boredom at bay. Mostly it was about keeping good community relationships with the locals. Helping out with petty crime, parking issues, and talking to the local schools. She had always wanted to be a local cop, part of the community, not set apart from it. Sarah had never longed for the big mysteries to solve, or the more detached role the bigger towns and cities police had. This role here was her dream job.

Of course, it didn't mean she would never have something big to deal with. A body being found here, on her patch, was a big deal. As the local policewoman, the big boys from town were relying on her to provide a bit of local flavor. It was something she could offer them with her eyes closed. She'd been stationed here in Port for four years now. She knew just about everybody who lived around here, by sight, at least. Pointing the detectives in the right direction when it came to speaking to members of the community who had been around for the last thirty years was easy. Sarah didn't have any first-hand experience of that time, being only just two weeks short of her thirty-second birthday.

The discovery of the body was something completely new. She'd had plenty of experience in that area, both here and in her previous postings in town. Usually, elderly people who had slipped away peacefully. Dealing with a corpse that had been buried underground was a completely new experience. It seemed unlikely there were going to be natural causes involved here, and it was bound to draw attention and interest from the whole country. There were reporters everywhere, calling the front desk, dropping in to ask questions, or accosting people on the street. Then there were the extra police officers in the station. Although the main incident room had been set up at the station in Dunedin, some detectives were working out of the Port Chalmers station. It seemed to make sense, seeing as there was plenty of room and it was close to the site of the discovery.

Sarah gathered together the paperwork she'd taken Helena's statement on. She had been reading through her notes and making sure nothing had been missed before handing it over to the detectives working on the case. She walked through the door into one of the back rooms. A few days ago, it had just been an unused space with some old office furniture stacked along one wall. The space had been a mess and could do with a good clean. Now the ancient chairs and desks had been pulled back in to use for the detectives using the room as their base. Looking around, Sarah saw some plain-clothes detectives sitting around, tapping away on laptops or talking on phones. She walked over to a desk in the corner and waited while Craig finished on his mobile phone.

He was a little older than Sarah, perhaps in his mid to late thirties. His hair was still dark, with no obvious signs of gray creeping in, but beginning to recede at the front and sides. It looked as though he had tried to keep the loss from becoming obvious by choosing a short haircut. Sarah had worked with him briefly in the past and while he clearly valued the local knowledge now, he always acted with a sense of superiority. He felt he was a cut above, with his detective role and position at the station in town, compared to Sarah with her small-town station and community policing.

There were a lot of empty takeout coffee cups on the desks. The detectives were clearly running on caffeine and very little else. Sarah tried not to be irritated by the mess they had made. It was unlikely they would be the ones to deal with it. Leaving the job for her once they'd finished here. Having the station busy might be nice, but it wasn't all perfect.

"Hi, Sarah," he said, putting the phone down and flashing what he no doubt felt was his winning smile. "Is that the witness statement?" He nodded toward the small sheaf of paper in her hand.

"Hi, Craig. Yes, Helena popped in about half an hour or so ago. I don't think there's anything to add to what she told us initially." Sarah handed the papers over to him and stood waiting while he skimmed through them. It had been surprising he hadn't wanted to interview Helena himself. But then, this wasn't like other suspicious deaths. Helena hadn't been on the scene when the death had happened and other than telling them about what the body had looked like when first discovered, something they had all seen for themselves, there wasn't much else. Helena wasn't a key witness, so he seemed to be more than happy to pass her witness interview off to someone else. Sarah suspected he might be a little less generous with anyone who had more vital information to share. Let him be protective of the important work—finding out what had happened was far more important than any glory in being the one to solve it all.

"Yeah, it's probably a good thing she did. It might have vanished under the slip again if she hadn't spotted it when she did. Or worse still, been found by a dog and dragged who knows where." He finished scanning the statement and slipped it away into a folder on the desk.

"Do we have any news on who it might be yet?" Sarah asked.

Craig turned on his chair to face her and leaned back slightly with his hands behind his head. It had been a long day for everyone, and he yawned and stretched before starting to talk. Sarah settled on the edge of a nearby desk. She couldn't help but be interested in this case and was as keen as anyone to hear what progress, if any, had been made.

"We're trying to narrow it down. There doesn't seem to be any record of any women going missing locally who would fit the age in the period we think it was buried. We're looking a bit further afield now, though. Someone must have an idea who she was and how she ended up there," he said. "I don't suppose you remember anyone ever talking about a woman going missing around here?"

"No," she said, trying once again to recall any conversation she'd ever had that might have mentioned a missing person. "It just doesn't make sense. If someone from around here had just vanished, I'm sure plenty of people would know something about it. It's just that kind of place."

He nodded and rubbed his hand over his face, the frustration clearly getting to him too. It was all so strange.

Maybe someone whose family didn't even know they had been here in Port Chalmers, or New Zealand for that matter. It didn't seem very likely someone could have gone missing who had traveled from another country. Surely there would have been a record of them missing or someone who had been worried when they didn't return. Records weren't as strict back then before the fear of terrorism influenced the way everything was done. People still needed passports and left a trail of some kind though, even thirty years ago.

"How far are you looking?" Sarah asked.

"Just within New Zealand to begin with. Then we'll look a bit further afield if there are no leads. There is only so much we can do if it turns out to be someone from overseas, though," Craig said.

"Will it take long to look into?"

"Not really. most people turn up within a few days of going missing. There are over three hundred people who are currently registered as missing in New Zealand, but for the period we're looking at it's much smaller, and then within in the age range and female, much smaller still." He shrugged. "In all honesty, I'm surprised we haven't got an idea of who it is already."

"There's no one that fits?" Sarah said. She had been expecting the identity to be discovered quite quickly.

"Nope. I'd think we'd got the time frame wrong, but the experts are pretty adamant it was between twenty-eight to thirty-two years ago. I even started looking five years either way and there's just no one. Even if it's someone who went missing long before they were killed or someone who wasn't reported for a couple of years after they vanished, there's still nothing."

Sarah frowned. It was all so strange. People didn't just vanish off the face of the earth and even if they did, people missed them. An unknown body turning up with no trace as to who it could belong to was almost unheard of.

"Was there anything on the body that might help identify them?" Sarah asked, glancing up at the wall, where photos of evidence had been displayed. Nothing obvious stood out. Craig followed her gaze and shook his head.

"No, there were some bits of clothing left, but most of it had broken down. We're trying to identify it now, to see if we can narrow down the shop it came from. That should give us an idea of where she's from. If she's wearing clothing that doesn't come from New Zealand or wasn't available here, then we might be able to get a better idea of where she came from, or at least where she had been. There was nothing else though, no jewelry or other personal belongings."

Sarah wandered closer to the wall, looking

carefully at the photos. The body itself was little more than bones, it didn't look like a body at all. But, once upon a time, this had been a living, breathing woman. She must have touched someone's life. She had to be someone. Someone knew something about her, Sarah felt sure of it.

"Do we know how she died?" Sarah asked, turning back to face Craig again.

He shook his head.

"It's hard to say. Bones were quite damaged, but that could have been caused after death. It may have been a strike to the head, or it could be something we can't see any trace of. We've got some scientists from the Uni having a closer look, but it's difficult with a skeleton that's been in the ground for this long."

He wandered over to join her at the board and they stood together looking at the crime scene photos for a minute. Silently searching for a missing clue or piece of evidence that hadn't been spotted yet, but there was nothing. Craig shook his head as he looked at the photos.

"It's been thirty years and there's very little evidence to go on. They'll keep us looking into it for a bit longer, but unless something turns up in the next few weeks, there's every chance this will just become one of those cold cases that get filed away and forgotten about," he said.

"It's just so frustrating. This just isn't the kind of thing that happens around here, and I hate the thought of it just being left," Sarah said.

"I know," he agreed, "I don't like to leave things unsolved either, but you know there's only a limited budget for policing, and cases that we stand a chance of cracking get priority."

He walked back to his desk, sat, and started to tap away on the laptop. Sarah gave a frustrated sigh. The sooner everything was all wrapped up and things could get back to normal in her small town and police station, the better. She couldn't help but worry if it remained unsolved, its shadow might hang over the community for years to come. The quiet community she loved so much might be lost forever.

Chapter 6

Deciding not to think about something anymore and not doing it were two very different things Helena soon discovered. It was hard not to wonder who the woman was and how she'd ended up buried in the bank at Back Beach. Although there had not been any further contact with the police or anyone involved in the investigation, the thought of what she had seen and found still hovered at the back of her mind. Nearly a week had passed since the interview at the police station.

With the police not having shared any new developments, it had dropped from the headlines, moving to the smaller articles later in the news and then to not being mentioned at all. At first glance, the thing that brought it back to her thoughts seemed completely unrelated to what had happened. One of the names on a poster on the supermarket noticeboard jumped out. It was someone that Greta from the library had mentioned when they were discussing the body. It didn't relate directly to what had been found, of course, but it stirred the interest.

Ordinarily, Helena wouldn't have given a local market another thought. However, she had more time on her hands to get involved. This market had the bonus of seeming to be the ideal way to do some digging, to see if it was possible to find out a little bit more about what had happened. Local community groups and committees were often the best way to find out all the local news and gossip around the town. Before there was a chance to overthink it, Helena tapped the contact details into her mobile phone. Taking a photo of the poster for good measure, modern technology made this kind of thing so much easier.

Fundraising Fair

18th August 1-4 pm

In aid of cancer research.

We are looking for extra help on the day.

Call Bill Harding 021200747 to volunteer or book a stall.

It seemed providential to see the poster today. Bill Harding was the name that Greta had mentioned, she was sure of it. The man who lived up in one of the houses opposite those that backed onto where the body had been found. From what Greta had said, he'd been very willing to talk about what was going on. Maybe he had heard something more, living so close to the action. If he had been involved with the community back when the body had gone into the ground, he might even remember something that might reveal some answers. Even if he didn't, maybe Helena could do her bit for the local community, volunteering in the name of a good cause. It was a win-win, although whether David would agree, or see through her flimsy reasoning remained to be seen.

As she tucked the phone back into her pocket, she couldn't help but shake her head. So much for forgetting about it and moving on. She wasn't fooling anyone, least of all herself, if she pretended that this was just some kind of volunteer fervor. Hopefully,

Dave wouldn't be too concerned about poking her nose in where she shouldn't.

****

Later that day, Helena arrived at the hall, which stood in the center of the town. Various community groups used one of several meeting places. It stood on the main road, almost right next to the police station. Helena had spoken to Bill briefly on the phone and he'd enthusiastically encouraged her to come along to the meeting this afternoon. Whether it was the fact that few other people seemed to have offered their services, or he was always this happy to get more help remained to be seen. Either way, the tentative quest to find out more had quickly morphed into becoming properly involved in the fair. It seemed she was going to become an active volunteer.

Despite walking passed it many times before, Helena had never actually been in the hall. Rather dark and gloomy, the small windows around the sides didn't allow much light to filter in and she had a hard time imagining it being a welcoming venue for community events. She blinked several times to get accustomed to the darkness. The gloomy winter day barely penetrated the room and, as of yet, the lights had not been turned on. The floor and walls were covered in dark wood adding to the dingy feeling.

As she stepped through the door and looked around, someone flipped on the light switch and suddenly the whole place transformed, the light reflecting off the wooden panels on the wall and the polished wooden floor. They felt warm, giving the place a cozy feel and what had felt unwelcoming magically transformed into a place people would want to spend time in. It was easy to imagine with a few people in here it would be different. It felt big enough for a party of at least a hundred or so people, and yet would still be quite intimate. Little furniture stood in the room. A few chairs were piled along the sides and tables were stacked in one corner, to the side of the raised stage area at one end of the hall. There were a few chairs set around a trestle table in the center of the room, ready for the meeting to begin. Helena walked toward them, looking around to see who had turned on the lights.

"Hi," said a voice from the corner of the room. "You must be Helen."

"Helena, yes," she replied.

A man walked forward with his hand held out, ready to shake hands, and a broad smile on his face. Helena guessed he would be in his seventies, although gauging ages wasn't something she really claimed as a talent. The small amount of hair he still had at the sides of his head had turned a soft gray color, but for the most part, he had lost his hair and the light shone on the top of his head giving the impression he had been without much hair for quite some years. Around Helena's height, perhaps slightly shorter, and although not a big man, he certainly wasn't slim. His eyes twinkled, and Helena found herself immediately at ease with him. Something about him brought to mind her grandfather and it was impossible but smile back at him. Dressed in dark trousers, a soft-looking pale shirt and a tie, he obviously came from a generation that believed in dressing smartly at all times.

"I'm Bill," he said, grasping her hand and giving it a firm shake. "Caretaker of this hall, for my sins, and general dogsbody. I'm also running this fundraising fair we're having. I understand you want to join in and help us out. Always on the lookout for new blood."

"Nice to meet you. Am I a bit early?" Helena replied, looking around at the otherwise empty hall.

Bill glanced at his watch.

"Only a touch. The others will be here any minute. We haven't got a lot to get through, but I thought it would give you a good idea of what's happening and where you'd like to get involved."

Helena felt swept along by the force of his personality, and realized he was a man of action, capable of achieving anything he set his mind to. No wonder he was in charge of running a fundraising fair, and no doubt many other kinds of things. He seemed like the kind of man people didn't say no to, and he spent his days organizing people and sorting things out.

"Sounds good," she said, following him to the table that had been set out for the meeting.

"Can I get you tea or coffee?" he asked, after indicating she should sit at the table. He walked toward the kitchen area at the back of the hall as he spoke.

"Yes, a cup of coffee would be lovely, thanks. White, no sugar, thanks."

Helena settled herself down and waited. A few minutes later, Bill returned with two brown glass mugs the type halls and community groups always seemed to have. He placed one down in front of Helena before sitting at the table and then taking a sip of his own.

"You saw our poster at the supermarket, then?" Bill asked,

"Yes, I've been looking for something to get involved with locally. My department has reduced my hours and I've got a bit more time to do this kind of thing," Helena said with a nod.

"Oh, you live locally then?" Bill talked as he pulled out papers from the old-fashioned doctor's bag he had brought with him, setting them on the table in front of him.

"Yes, Sawyers Bay. We've been there for over twenty years now, but I haven't had much time to get involved until now." Helena couldn't help but defend herself, feeling guilty she hadn't been involved in things before now, especially when faced with someone like Bill, who no doubt gave up his time for all kinds of good causes.

"Well, it's good to have you on board. It's always good to have a few new faces. People are so busy with work, we struggle to get people involved these days."

"Thanks, I'm looking forward to finally getting involved in something."

"You can only do what you can do and you're here now," he said with a smile. He turned toward the opening of the door. "That sounds like the others now."

Helena turned toward the door as well to see the newcomers arrive. Two women, both in their late sixties, Helena guessed, came in and walked over to their table.

"Oh, you here already, Bill," the one of them with light brown hair said.

"When isn't he? He's always the first to arrive and the last to leave," the other woman commented with a laugh. She had darker, wavy hair and a broad smiling face.

Helena could feel the two women looking at her and sizing her up. They didn't come right and out to ask who she was and why she was sitting there with Bill, but the unasked question hung in the air. They quickly pulled off their coats and made themselves comfortable, each sending Helena a small nod of greeting as she sat there waiting for the meeting to begin.

"We've got a new willing helper to join our happy band today, ladies," Bill said once they were ready and settled. He smiled broadly toward Helena. "This is Helena, and she's looking to give us a hand."

"Hi, I'm Cathy," said the lady with the darker wavy hair, nodding toward Helena with a tight smile.

"Nice to meet you, I'm Diane," said the other woman.

"Hi," Helena replied, smiling at each of them in turn.

Although they seemed to be friendly enough when greeting her, Helena got the distinct impression they were less than thrilled to have her there. She wondered how long the two women had been the only ones attending Bill's meetings and helping to run his events. Bill might be pleased to have new blood along to help out, but she wasn't sure it was a sentiment shared by the other members of the committee.

"Right, down to business," said Bill, bringing the meeting to order.

By the end of the meeting, Helena found herself in charge of the bookstall at the coming weekend fair. She had hoped she could just lend some moral support or help someone else out who had been involved in the past, but somehow, she found herself agreeing to run a whole stall by herself. Bill was clearly the driving force behind the group, meeting little resistance to his suggestions. There was no chance he wasn't going to find her a job straight away. The fair was clearly his brainchild, with most of the ideas and suggestions coming from him, with little input from the other members of the group. Helena suspected the two other women were there primarily because they enjoyed his gentle flirting and organizational skills rather than any deep conviction for the cause they were raising funds for. Bill had an easy charm, which helped him to get people on his side and do jobs for him. It also seemed to have helped him build his little fan club of middle-aged women.

"Thanks for your help," he said as Helena helped him to pack away the table and chairs. Cathy and Diane had already scurried home and Helena decided it was the prime opportunity to see if she could introduce the subject of the body.

"No problem, I've been looking for something to get involved in locally," she said.

"No husband at home to look after?" Bill asked.

They had just lifted and carried the table to the stack in the corner. Helena blew out a breath and leaned on it for a second. They were heavier than they looked.

"Oh yes, but he looks after himself, or we do it between us. I've never really been, or wanted to be, much of a housewife," she said with a little laugh. Bill shook his head, but she didn't feel he disapproved.

"Ah yes, of course, modern marriage. My wife was much more traditional. She cooked, cleaned, and did most things around the house while I worked. Of course, it's a long time since I've had a woman around the house to do those things," he said with a depreciating chuckle and a slight smile.

"You're not married anymore?"

"No, she passed away nearly thirty years ago. God rest her soul."

Helena grimaced. Had Greta mentioned that? She couldn't remember much of what had been said. The body seemed far more interesting at the time. It was one of those little facts about people she liked to try and remember to avoid awkwardness and embarrassment. Even if a bereavement wasn't recent, it was good to know beforehand and avoid bringing up something that might be painful.

"Oh, I am sorry, I hadn't realized."

"It's been a long time now." He turned toward her and patted her shoulder, as though she was the one in need of comfort. "Life carries on."

He didn't seem to be too upset, Helena noted with relief. She didn't want to get off on the wrong foot with him by saying the wrong thing. They walked toward the entrance to the hall together. Bill turned the lights off when they reached the door.

"Do you need a lift home?" she asked. "Or did you drive?"

"Thank you, that would be lovely. I walked down, but the walk back up the hill is always less appealing. I live up on Magnetic Street, so it shouldn't be too far out of your way."

Helena nodded. Many of the streets around Port Chalmers were steep and weren't always that welcoming to walk back up. She led the way to her car. This would be the ideal opportunity to bring up the body.

"You must have been fairly close to the action the other day with the body that was found," Helena began, pulling away from the curb.

"Yes, well, I couldn't see anything from my house, but it's the houses just down the road which back onto that area. Not that they'd have had anything to do with it, I can't imagine." He knew instantly what she was referring to and Helena was glad she hadn't had to go into more detail to introduce the topic. It was hardly surprising; it was all that had been spoken about in the town for the last week.

"No, I gather it had been there for quite a long time." Helena paused. Did she own up to having been the one who had found it, or just keep quiet? She wanted to know more, to find out if Bill did know anything, but at the same time, she didn't want her part known to everyone. There had been some attempt by reporters to cover the story, but Helena hadn't come across anywhere where they had mentioned her by name. The local gossip would soon no doubt out her, but perhaps Bill had not made the connection as yet. She had been quite relieved to have been left out of things and wanted to keep things that way. Before she could decide whether to probe further, Bill decided for her.

"It makes you wonder though, doesn't it," he said, "who she was and how she ended up there."

"It does, poor thing. Someone must have missed her or loved her once. To just end up buried there with no trace, only to be discovered because the ground slips away…"

Once again, Helena could see the bones protruding from the ground as they had been when she first saw them last week. The white bone stood out against the dull red-brown of the muddy bank. She shivered thinking about it. Bill didn't seem to notice her discomfort.

"We'll probably never know though. I don't think the police have had any joy finding out who she is," Bill said.

"No, I hadn't heard they had. I'm not sure they would have said much on the news though. They tend to keep things to themselves while they're investigating, don't they?"

"I've got an old friend who was in the force. He still keeps in touch with the local police. He was telling me just the other day they hadn't had any leads. This is my place, just up here."

The house he pointed out was a small and well-looked-after bungalow with cream-painted weatherboards on the walls and a well-established section full of bushes and trees.

"This one with the lovely garden?" she asked, pulling over just outside.

"Yes, that's the one. I like to keep it nice, keeps me busy. Well, thanks again for the lift. I'll see you at the weekend."

"Great, see you then. Unless there's anything else you need me to do in the meantime?" Helena wanted to try and keep the conversation going in the hope he might tell her something more, assuming there was anything else to tell.

"Now you mention it. There is something. There's a farm up toward Pūrākaunui I need something dropping off at if you don't mind. I'll just go and get it."

Bill walked away into his house and emerged a moment later carrying a brown cardboard folder of documents.

"It's not anything to do with the fair. It's for the local history group. But seeing as you've got a car and I tend to find all of these local things are all tied in one way or another, so if you don't mind?" He handed the folder through the window to her. "It's just a few local history bits and pieces from a family that's been here generations. The local history group that uses the hall borrowed them recently and asked me to drop them off. I would, but my car has been off the road recently and, well, to be honest with you, John and I don't exactly see eye to eye. The address is there on the front."

She took the cardboard folder from him, placing it on the front seat of the car.

"Yes, of course, that's no problem. I haven't been out that way for a while. It will be a nice drive."

"Thanks so much. I think he might have some more bits and pieces for us. Old photos and the like. Feel free to have a look through them. They can be quite interesting to those of us who know the area now." He moved away from the open car window, waving as she got ready to drive away. "I'll see you at the weekend, then."

Helena drove off. Bill was an interesting character. Even if this didn't help to find out more about the body, it had been entertaining to meet him. She could see how he managed to organize his groups, getting people to do things and help him out was a well-honed skill and one he wasn't shy to employ. Not that she minded—she'd offered to help out and a drive out to Pūrākaunui was always a welcome trip.

Chapter 7

Helena drove up over the hills and out of Port Chalmers to the north. The view over the coast was breathtaking. Even on a day like today, with the clouds hanging low and heavy in the sky. They created a dramatic backdrop to the coastline and seascape, which in some ways enhanced the view. The dark sky made the land and sea stand out sharply, and the sea in the distance had white tips of spray, whipped up by the wind. It was wild enough that the movement of the water could be seen even from a distance.

The weather had been just as wild here over the last few weeks as it had been at home. Parts of the road had suffered slips and a large section had been closed, but for the most part, things had been repaired now and were back open. Getting nearer to the small communities of Long Beach, Pūrākaunui and Osborne, the road was more exposed. It ran high above the coastline, with an uninterrupted view back toward Port Chalmers and out to the ocean in the other direction. The weather attacked it more ferociously, but somehow this seemed to keep it safer. There were few trees to fall and block the route and the road had nowhere to slip away to. All the damage that could have been done took place long ago, leaving a weathered but secure road.

She hadn't been up this way for a while, since her children were young. They had sometimes gone to

Murderer's Beach or Long Beach to paddle in the sea or play on the sand. Now, it was just her and David at home, and a beach trip wasn't something she often did. On occasion, she did drive out toward Aramoana, which was closer. The road was winding, but mostly well-maintained, being the only route to the rest of the world for the people who lived out here. The directions Bill had given her were easy to follow and no need to travel all the way into the small settlement of Pūrākaunui. The house in question was on the main road itself and she wouldn't have to spend a lot of time hunting for it down little lanes and tracks. She soon spotted the house, set back from the road but with a commanding view out over the sea and surrounding area.

Up here, the strong wind gave the property a wild, exposed feeling. A modern building, the farmhouse lacked the homely feeling some of the older homesteads seemed to have. There was little attempt to build a garden around it and Helena did not feel she, or any other visitor for that matter, was welcome, even before she'd met anyone. Helena drove along the rough stone driveway and stopped in front of the house. There were a few farm buildings off to one side and an old, tumbledown house up on a small hill behind the current farmhouse. Presumably, this is where the farmer's family had lived when they first started to work and live here. Much of the land had been in some families' hands for generations. Those who stayed slowly bought up surrounding properties and increased the size of their farms.

She climbed out of the car and looked around for a sign of life. There didn't seem to be anyone around, but there were cars parked by the house and with smoke coming out of the chimney, it looked as though a fire had been lit inside. Getting closer, only one of the cars looked as though it was still in use. The others had an old, abandoned feel to them, as though no one had attempted to start them for some years. Even the one potentially still running was an older model car, one that looked like it had been in use for some years. It did seem clean and well maintained, while the other cars had begun to rust and the weeds growing around the wheels suggested they hadn't moved in a long time.

Perhaps this hadn't been the best idea. It was an isolated and lonely place, and here she was visiting a man she'd never met before. It had seemed like a good idea when Bill had suggested it, but she might have been too hasty. 'Shuddering as discomfort took root. Surely Bill wouldn't have sent her if there was anything to be concerned about.

Helena walked up the three steps onto the concrete veranda wrapped around the right side of the property and knocked on the door at the front. It was a 70's built house by the looks of things, squat and ugly in the beautiful landscape, function over form. The front door was textured glass, with a picture of a stag etched into it. Perhaps not the most decorative of items, but it stopped her from being able to see properly into the house. The woodwork around it was painted in faded yellow and, although it wasn't peeling, the sun had bleached it over time into almost white in places. Helena turned and stood looking out at the view, waiting for someone to answer the door. From here she could see the sea at Long Beach and right down the coastline in both directions. This might be an unforgiving place to live during the winter months, but it was breathtakingly beautiful.

Someone was moving around inside, so she knocked again. This time, someone walked toward the door. It opened and a tall man, who looked as though he must be in his early sixties, looked at her. His hair was short, wispy, and gray, although he still had plenty. He wore a blue checked work shirt and jeans, which were well-worn. He gave off the impression of a man used to working out in the elements. His face was tanned and weathered from years spent outside. As she looked at him, Helena wondered if he really was as old as she had first guessed.

"Can I help you?" the man said with a frown. He probably thought she was trying to sell him something.

"Hi, yes. Are you John? I've been asked to drop these papers off to you." She held out the folder that Bill had given her with a tentative smile, not sure how he would respond to some strange woman turning up on his doorstep.

"Oh, from the local history group? Come in, I've got some more for you to take back." His face broke into a wide smile, surprising Helena, having not expected the owner of the house to be quite so welcoming. It seemed at odds with the way the place looked from the outside.

"Thank you," Helena replied, following him into the warm house. The intention had been to drop the folder off and leave, but the idea of standing out on the cold doorstep while waiting for him to dig out the new documents didn't appeal. The opportunity to see what the house was like inside and to find out more about him was too appealing to resist.

"I didn't realize there were some more to collect," Helena said, heading into the comfortable-looking lounge area.

"Yes, I found some more of my sister's papers. Local history and our family tree were quite an interest for Jessie at one point. I came across them the other day and thought the historical society might be interested. Now, where did I put them?"

There were piles of paperwork around the room—on the ends of bookshelves, on the small coffee tables, and on other available surfaces. The room wasn't untidy, but it bulged with things. A cozy and comfortable room, with an old brown enameled log burner throwing out a welcoming heat. The décor was old and dated, although well looked after and clean.

"I suppose Bill has got you running around for him?" he asked, turning his head back as he hunted for the papers.

"Um, yes."

"He's good at that. Getting people, women that is, to do things for him." The tone of censure in his voice made Helena feel slightly uncomfortable. Even if Bill hadn't warned the two men didn't quite see eye to eye, it would soon have become obvious there was some bad feeling here. Coming here might have been a mistake.

"I don't know him. I just fancied a drive out here, haven't been for a while, so said I'd help out. I'm just volunteering at a local fair," she quickly explained, somehow feeling as though she'd been caught doing something she shouldn't. "You don't get on?"

He sighed and didn't answer as he continued to shuffle through the piles of paper looking for his sister's local history papers. It didn't seem as though he was going to reply to her, when he suddenly straightened up, holding a brown cardboard folder.

"He's just a bit full of himself. He's got rental properties all over Port Chalmers and thinks it makes him a bit of a cut above the rest of us. I haven't seen him for years. We used to be friendly, well of a sort, but after Jessie left, well, things just weren't the same between us anymore."

"Jessie?" Who was he talking about?

"My sister. She left, must be nearly thirty years ago now. Left all kinds of strife behind her, but that was Jessie for you. It's all well and good being carefree and light-hearted, but it's not real life. Those of us who've got to get on with everything are just left picking up the pieces."

Helena nodded, trying to look contrite. Almost as though she were the one being chastised for lifestyle choices, even though he knew nothing of her, and if she was being honest, carefree wasn't something she associated with herself. John certainly knew nothing of the way she lived.

"Don't listen to me. I'm a bitter old man with too much thinking time on his hands. Everyone loved Jessie and I think she just couldn't cope with it anymore. I don't blame her for leaving, would have done it myself if I hadn't got the responsibility of this place on my hands."

Helena turned and looked out of the window at the farmland he indicated.

"It's a beautiful spot you've got here." A subject change from something he obviously still found painful seemed to be a good idea.

"It is. At one time it was a big farm. It's just me

now, with no one to pass it on to and I've sold much of the land off. I haven't farmed it for years, just a couple of animals for the freezer. Jessie wasn't keen on getting involved in the farming, and she wouldn't have kept the land either."

He handed Helena the folder and walked back across the room toward the archway at the back.

"I suppose it wasn't that interesting for a young girl?" Helena asked.

"No, and she had all of these big dreams. Jessie planned to take on the world. Well, maybe the male half, anyway," he said with a chuckle.

"She had a few boyfriends then?" Helena said, returning his smile.

"Just a few. She liked male attention, but one man was never enough. Even back at school, she'd have a whole gang following her around. It caused a few issues between me and my mates." He shook his head, lost in the past. "I thought maybe she'd settle down with Murray, but even when she was with him, he wasn't the only one. Probably the best thing. I was never very keen on him. Would you like a coffee while you're here?" he asked with a sudden change of subject.

"Yes, please, that would be lovely." Helena hadn't planned to stay. John seemed to be a bit lonely out here on his own and he seemed willing to chat. "Murray? Who was that?"

"A local mechanic. Jessie was quite serious about him for a while. Once she left, he didn't stick around himself, cleared off somewhere. I wondered if he'd followed her, but I don't know. Either way, she went and now I'm the last one here at the farm." He headed into the kitchen and Helena could hear him moving around, filling the jug and making a drink. He returned a moment later with a tray, a couple of mugs, a bottle of milk and a sugar bowl. It seemed almost like something from another time. Nobody usually bothered with that kind of set up these days. A hot drink at a friend's was usually just a mug of instant coffee, or if they were really fancy, a coffee from a pod machine.

"I wasn't sure how you liked it, so I thought you could do that bit yourself," he said, sitting on one of the armchairs and putting the tray down on the little table in the center of the room.

"Thanks," Helena said, sitting on the other armchair and adding milk to the coffee. She glanced up at him. "Your sister didn't have a family? Some kids who might come back and help out?"

"I don't know. I haven't seen her since she left. I don't know if she met someone and settled down, or what happened to her."

A slight suspicion began to grow in Helena's mind.

"You haven't heard from her in thirty years?"

John took a sip of his coffee and then gazed off into the distance, looking at something from the past only he could see. He was quiet for a moment and then finally answered.

"Oh no, she used to send a postcard every year, stopped a couple of years ago, must have got tired of it or something."

He indicated the mantelpiece, which stood over the enamel wood stove by the far wall. Helena stood and wandered over, picking up the stack of postcards sitting there. Flicking through them, looking at the holiday scenes on the front. Each one showed a different tourist scene from somewhere in Australia. They were from all over the country and were just the generic cards you could find in most tourist shops all over the world. Selecting one at random, she turned it over.

John, all good here in Oz. Hope all is well with you. Much love, Jessie x

The message seemed fairly impersonal, not the kind of thing you might expect from someone who had left the country with no plans of returning home. The cards were dated roughly once a year, going back over the past thirty years or so. Each one carried a similar message—no further details. Helena placed them carefully back on the mantelpiece.

"I don't know why I keep them really," John said, now standing and watching as she looked at them.

"Sorry. I wasn't meaning to be nosy. I just couldn't imagine someone leaving and only sending postcards."

"Jessie was never big on writing. The early ones were to Dad and me when he was still alive, but they didn't say anything more. Then once Dad died, they were written just to me."

"She knew your father had died then?"

"Yes. I hadn't thought about it before, but the year after Dad died, the card was just to me. She must have been in touch with someone locally to tell her, but she didn't come to the funeral. I thought she might come back once it was just me, but she never has."

Helena nodded. There was something about this that seemed important. Perhaps just the coincidence of someone leaving around the same time the body had been buried, although it could have been a couple of years difference for all anyone knew.

"And one still arrived every year after your dad died? Even though Jessie never came back?" Helena asked.

"No, I haven't had one for the last three or four years now. I'm not sure why they stopped. Probably thought there was no point anymore. Not when she didn't call or visit."

Helena nodded, thinking there didn't seem to be anything here to do with the body, just a bit of a coincidence. They both sat there in silence for a few minutes, each lost in their thoughts. Helena hadn't intended to stay for more than a few minutes and yet here she sat chatting to John and stopping for a drink.

"Well, thank you for the coffee and the folder." She stood up and picked up the folder he'd given her. "I'd better be getting on and leave you in peace."

"Don't worry about it. It's nice to have someone to talk to for a change. Feel free to pop up and visit me again sometime. I enjoyed your company," he said with a smile. "If you feel like baking some biscuits or something I'm sure I can find a home for them."

She laughed as he winked at her, a twinkle appearing in his eyes giving a glimpse of what he might have been like as a younger man.

"Well, thanks for these anyway. I'll see if I can come by again soon. See you later."

Helena sat for a few moments in the car before driving away. She hadn't expected to stay at the house for so long. John seemed like a nice, but lonely man, old before his time perhaps. It was hard to imagine living out here with only yourself for company. Perhaps it didn't bother him, though. He wasn't someone she had noticed in Port Chalmers before, so it didn't seem he visited regularly, or perhaps he just wasn't noticeable. Still, she felt a bit sorry for him out here alone and decided to try to come and visit him again soon.

Then there was everything she had learned about his sister. Could there be some connection between Jessie and the body that had been found? They both seem to have been involved with something thirty years ago. She had started to wonder if Jessie was the girl who'd gone missing, but with all of those postcards on the mantelpiece, it didn't seem likely. Even so, it was a coincidence and perhaps there was some connection there. Perhaps she'd speak to Bill about Jessie and see if he knew anything about John's sister. Helena scrubbed her hands over her face. Why was she even bothering about this? The body, other than finding it, had nothing to do with her, and neither did John's sister for that matter. Thinking about this too much was surely a shortcut to madness. It was ancient history and probably should stay that way.

Chapter 8

"Something smells good," Helena called out as she walked through the door.

"Hey, good day?" David said, turning toward her from where he stood at the stove. He leaned forward and gave her a quick kiss. 'Thought we'd have Thai tonight."

"Sounds great, I'm starving. I've been out being community-minded. How's your day been?" she asked, dumping her bag on one of the chairs next to the kitchen table and pulling her jacket off.

"Same old, same old. Nothing new. So, you're embracing this being a local then? What have you got yourself roped into?" He grinned.

He poured her a glass of red wine and handed it over as she sat down at the table.

"I'm helping out with some fete or sale or something. It's on at the weekend. I met the organizer,' the kind you expect to be running that kind of thing."

"Sandals and a beard?"

"No," she said, laughing. "He just seems very capable and has all the local housewives wrapped around his little finger. He's one of those who've been at the heart of the community since the beginning of time and knows everyone and their business."

Helena couldn't help but be amused by David's suggestion. She couldn't imagine anyone less likely to be dressed in sandals with a beard. He had seemed too well turned out, neatly dressed and clean-shaven. He'd been wearing a shirt and tie, even though just attending a local committee meeting.

"You mean if you're involved locally yourself? Can't say I know him," David said.

"Well, yes, not like us lot who keep to ourselves."

He laughed. "You're becoming a proper pillar of the community. I'll have to watch out. You'll be showing me up with my lack of commitment to all important causes. Here I am letting the side down."

"We'll see. This is my first foray into committees and the like. I'm not sure how keen I'll be once I've had a taste of it. Let's get this weekend over and done with first."

David turned and began to dish out the meal he'd been cooking—Thai chicken curry with rice. The rich scents swirled around the kitchen and Helena's stomach rumbled in anticipation. She took a sip of the wine and flipped open the cover of the cardboard folder she'd brought in with her.

"What's that?" David asked, nodding toward the file as he placed the bowl down in front of her.

"Some local history stuff I agreed to pick up for Bill, the guy from the meeting. I went out to Pūrākaunui this afternoon. Met a farmer who had some things for the local history group. Nice guy."

"Pūrākaunui? Haven't been up there for ages," David said, sitting down at the table with his bowl of food.

"No, me either. He's got a lovely place, a view right out to the coast. It's all wild and rugged. Must be a bit lonely though, just him, no family. Enough to send anyone a bit odd." She took a bite of food. "This is delicious, by the way."

David reached over and looked at some of the things in the folder. He picked up a small pile of photos of various ages. Some were black and white prints from the early days of cameras, while others were more modern. These were color prints but had still faded with time, giving them a rather washed-out appearance.

"Are these all photos of the local area?" he asked, flipping through them.

"Yes, I think so. I haven't had a chance to look yet. There are some old newspaper clippings, photos, and letters, I think. Apparently, his sister was interested in them."

"Was? She's not into local history anymore?"

"No, she left and went to Australia thirty years or so ago now. John said he hadn't seen her since then. I think he must have been clearing out some of her things he'd kept hold of all this time and thought the local history group could use them or something." Helena continued to eat while David looked at the photos. The food was delicious and right now was far more interesting than some old photos.

"This must be the Port before they built the container terminal." He held out a photo to show her.

"Yes, I think so. I've seen some photos of it at the museum down in Port."

Helena reached over and picked up some photos, flicking through them. They were mostly pictures of buildings and landscapes, rather than of people. Despite their age, many of them were instantly recognizable as landmarks from Port Chalmers, even if some of the buildings had changed or even vanished over the years.

"Is this her?" David asked, holding up another photo. A young woman stood posing in front of Chick's Hotel in Port Chalmers. She looked to be in her late teens and was dressed in a short skirt and brightly colored t-shirt. The photo had faded through age, but the girl still looked vibrant and full of fun, even in a photograph with muted colors. She stood with one arm raised as though introducing the building behind her while laughing at whoever was taking the picture.

"I don't know," Helena said, taking the picture from him. She looked at it and flipped it over to see if anything had been written on the back, but it was blank. "I don't know what she looked like. It might be, or a friend of hers. They belonged to her, so I assume it might be Jessie, though."

There was something about the girl in the photo. She was smiling, happy, as though without a care in the world. Not the look of the kind of person who would just up and leave and run away from everything she had known before. Helena shook her head, reading far too much into an old snap. She'd got photos of the boys where they looked as though the world had ended, just because a balloon had popped or there was no ice cream, and five minutes later, they'd be smiling again. A photo was nothing more than a second-long glimpse into someone's life and a posed one at that—far from telling the whole picture. Besides, she couldn't be sure this even was Jessie. The building might have been the point, not the girl. The pub had long been a local landmark, even if no longer used to serve alcohol, it had been part of the community for a very long time.

Helena looked at the other pieces in the folder. There was a family tree for the Andrew's family, ending with John and Jessie. Had Jessie gone on to have children of her own? John certainly seemed to be the last of the male line. Their mother must have died when they were both young, judging by the date given on the family tree. His father had died twenty-six years ago, so Jessie must have left before that. She remembered John saying the postcards had been addressed to their father and John before he had died.

The other documents in the folder were a couple of old maps and street plans. Some documents seemed to relate to the Andrews' farm and its land. Plans of the area they had once owned, and notes added regarding who it had been sold to and when. At one time it must have been quite a large farm, but now only the small parcel of land that surrounded the farmhouse Helena visited today remained. There was also a plan for two houses in Port Chalmers. Perhaps they had been rental properties the family had owned at one time? There was nothing in the folder Helena thought might have had anything to do with the remains she discovered.

****

Later that evening, Helena sat and read through the contents of the folder more closely while David was busy marking some of his student's assignments. There was something about old photos that was fascinating, seeing how places had changed over the years. She picked up the picture of the girl again. Was this John's missing sister? Is that you Jessie? What happened to you? Something must have made her suddenly leave and never come back to see her family. It was true that the farm didn't seem like the kind of place a young woman would want to stay forever. But there was surely no need to go so far and for so long. John hadn't suggested it, but he must have had some kind of fall out with Jessie, something that had stopped her from getting back in touch all of these years, that made her up and leave in the first place. But what if she hadn't? It was an itch at the back of her mind that Helena couldn't quite dismiss.

"Dave, you don't think this Jessie could be my body, do you? The one I found, I mean. No one's seen her for around thirty years."

"Hmm, I did wonder when you mentioned her. But didn't you say she'd been sending postcards from Australia?" he asked, looking up from his work and pushing the reading glasses 'on top of his head.

"Oh, of course, I'd forgotten about that." She rubbed her hands over her eyes and shook her head. "I don't know why but I can't help feeling there's some kind of connection here. Which is silly, why should there be?"

"It's just because you feel involved, that and the fact you watch too many detective programs on TV, of course," he said with a laugh. "You're expecting there to be some connection because you've found out about Jessie at the same time you've found this body. That's how it works in those TV shows."

"Oh, very funny. I'm sure you'd be completely disinterested if you'd found her."

"No, of course, and you know I'm joking. Do you fancy a coffee?" He got up from the chair and put the papers he'd been marking down on the coffee table in front of him.

"Thanks," she said, flicking through the papers again. There didn't seem to be anything else in there that would help her. She'd have to speak to Bill about

Jessie when they met tomorrow. He knew John and no doubt his sister too, even if they didn't get on with one another. Perhaps whatever had made Jessie leave was in some way connected to the girl who had died? Maybe Jessie and a friend had got into some kind of argument and there had been some kind of accident or something. Surely someone else would have known something about that and there would have been two women of a similar age going missing. No, it didn't make sense either.

Putting away the papers, Helena picked up her mobile phone and opened up Facebook. She wasn't sure it would help, but it was worth a try. She tried Jessie Andrews first. It brought up a few people called Jessica, but none of them looked as though they would be about the right age, and they weren't in Australia or New Zealand. She would be in her late forties or early fifties by now surely. How old had she been when she left? Her late teens, early twenties? The women it brought up were all much younger. She might have married and changed her name in the last thirty years anyway. If she wanted to stay undiscovered, she might have even adopted a new first name. It was a silly thought. Not everyone was even on Facebook, after all. Before setting down her phone, Helena brought up an internet browser and searched for Jessie Andrews in the search engine and then Jessica Andrews. There were pages and pages of hits, but a cursory glance of the first few pages revealed nothing that seemed to be about the Jessie she was looking for. Even adding Australia or New Zealand to the search terms didn't help bring anything helpful up.

Helena frowned and wondered what to look for

next. What about the boyfriend John had mentioned, Murray something or other? She couldn't search for him online without a surname or more details, but John had mentioned him being a mechanic. If he'd worked at the local garage, there was a chance they could remember him there and might be able to tell her more. She added a trip to the garage to her mental list for the morning. Helena shook her head and felt like laughing at herself. She might have planned to get more involved in the community, but this was taking it to some kind of extreme.

"Still no joy?" David asked, handing her the cup of coffee he'd just made.

"Thanks, love. No, nothing. I'm going to give up for now. I thought I might ask Bill when I see him tomorrow. He seems to know everyone."

"Well just be careful. People can get a bit funny when you go and rake up ancient history. You've only just met this guy and you don't want to upset him too much," he said with a slight frown.

"Don't worry, I can be discreet when I want to be." She winked. "Is there anything on TV?"

Chapter 9

Saturday morning arrived. The weather had cleared up a little over the last week and as Helena parked outside the hall she wondered if this might bring more people along to have a look. The fete would be held in the same hall they held their previous meeting. Helena arrived in time to set up her stall before everything started.

"Morning. Where do you want me?" she called out to Cathy and Diane as she entered the hall. They were busy setting up their stalls on the trestle tables that someone had already erected around the edge and in the center of the room.

"Morning, Helena," Cathy replied. "Yours are the tables over there to the back of the hall." She gestured vaguely behind herself. "Bill's dropped off most of the books, so you can start setting them out if you want to. He'll be back soon."

Helena looked toward where Cathy had pointed and saw several banana boxes and other cardboard containers stacked alongside a table at the back of the hall. An array of second-hand books in various shapes, sizes, and colors in them, all thrown in haphazardly, rather than sorted in any way.

"Thanks. He won't need any help with bringing things in?" she asked while making her way to the books.

"No, he's got some Scouts helping with the heavy lifting. He said he'd be back at around eleven with floats and the like for later," Cathy said. "He's always got things sorted before we start. I think he's had to go and do some work on one of his rental properties first. Something about a tap leaking, I think."

Helena began to sort through and move around the heavy boxes full of books. Someone had been busy earlier on, dropping them off, as there was more than enough to fill the stall with just about every genre or topic imaginable. There were even a few Helena decided might be best left at the bottom of the pile or even left off the stall entirely, particularly those of a sensitive nature, while others were past their best with torn pages or scribbles on them. She hadn't been particularly looking forward to the fair, but now, with the task of sorting the books into some kind of order, she soon found herself swept along by the work and taking pride in the stall. There was something strangely satisfying about grouping the books attractively on the stall. Making sure the selection looked interesting and would invite people to browse through them. About half an hour must have passed when Cathy wandered over to see how she was getting on. Standing slightly back, she watched Helena work with the superior air of someone who had plenty of experience in this kind of thing.

"Books are quite easy," Cathy commented, peering into the top of the boxes. "People like to browse. There's something a bit more respectable about second-hand books than there is clothing or bric-a-brac. Most people don't mind second-hand books. They don't usually have that used smell either, if you know what I mean." Cathy wrinkled her nose.

Cathy was manning the cake stall; she'd made it quite clear at the previous meeting that she wanted nothing to do with anything second-hand that had been donated. Happy to help out for a charitable cause, as long as she didn't need to deal with anything she felt was somehow beneath her. Giving the appearance of helping without stepping too far out of her comfort zone. Fortunately, a couple of volunteers Helena hadn't met before seemed to have been willing to take on those roles and were now busy laying out the clothing and crockery, pots, pans, and other oddments that made up the second-hand stalls.

Diane drifted over to join Cathy at Helena's stall and the two of them had started to look through the boxes of books together, commenting on the various titles they came across. Cathy picked up a book on the history of Port Chalmers and started flicking through it.

"Oh, are you interested in local history, then?" Helena asked, nodding toward the book, "Are you part of Bill's local history group?"

"Me? Not really." Cathy returned the book to the box. "But my husband Frank used to be quite keen and in the group. I haven't got out of the habit of looking for things for him, even though he's been dead a few years now."

"I don't suppose you stop thinking about things they would have liked, though," Helena replied with a small, sad smile. "I'm sorry to hear he's dead. You must miss him."

Cathy didn't answer and Helena got the impression she didn't seem to want to follow this line of conversation, so Helena changed the subject to something she wanted to know a bit more about. Especially seeing as there was a connection to what they had just been discussing.

"I went up to see John Andrew's farm the other day. He'd got some local history things for Bill. I suppose your husband would have known him?"

"Yes, well, we all know John. Or we did. He used to be a lot more involved in things around here. Before. Keeps to himself these days," Cathy said.

"He doesn't tend to come down into town unless he has to these days," added Diane.

"He seemed nice. Showed me some photos and things." Helena paused. "There was one of his sister, but I think he said she's not been around much recently."

"Her!?" Cathy bristled. "That little cow!"

Helena was taken aback by the violence of Cathy's reaction. She didn't know what she had expected, but it certainly wasn't the sudden blast of dislike and ill-feeling she was now faced with.

"You didn't like her, I take it?" Helena asked.

"Not at all. Full of herself, she was, and out to catch a man. Didn't matter who the man was or whose' man he was, for that matter, she wanted them all. Fortunately, my Frank had far more sense than to get sucked in by her. That's more than most of them did. All over her, they were. Pathetic." Cathy almost spat the words as she spoke.

"Sorry, I didn't know her. She was before my time here," Helena said quickly, wanting to smooth over what seemed to be an unpleasant memory of the girl.

"Cleared off years ago, she did. Good riddance. Probably knew no one wanted her back here again."

With that, Cathy stalked back off to her cake stall. Helena almost felt bad for bringing it up. There was still a lot of bad feeling around Jessie, even after all these years. It was pretty clear something had happened between Jessie and Cathy's husband, perhaps made even more obvious by the amount she protested.

"She was never a fan of the girl," Diane said in an undertone to Helena. She had been standing quietly there the whole time Cathy had been talking, not getting involved in the conversation while Cathy had still been there. "I'm not sure if it was jealousy for all the attention she got or something more."

Helena looked at her questioningly, raising her eyebrows.

"Oh, quite the looker in her day, Cathy was. She was getting older by the time Jessie was around though. I don't think she liked the idea of some younger woman getting all the attention from the men. Especially not her men," Diane said with a significant look.

"Her men?"

"Yes, well her husband, obviously, but she's always had a bit of a thing about Bill too."

Helena looked over to Cathy. She was talking to Bill, laughing at something he had said. While she wasn't quite flirting with him, there was something almost proprietorial about the way she stood next to him as he talked to other people. Yes, she could see that there was some kind of connection there.

"Jessie and Cathy had a big bust-up back then, just before Jessie went missing. Cathy accused her of flirting with Frank, and Jessie said Cathy was only sticking with Frank because Bill wouldn't have her. It was all nonsense, of course. Bill's wife died somewhere around then, and Cathy had never made any sign she'd like to be with Bill. Even now, when Frank's been dead for years himself."

With that revelation, Diane nodded and headed back to her own stall, where she was serving tea and coffee next to the cake stall. It was the most Helena had heard Diane say since she had met her. She'd almost dismissed the other woman as being shy and quiet, but it wasn't the whole story. When Cathy was around, Diane was happy to take a back seat, but there was a mischievous side to her that seemed to relish some juicy gossip. Even at the expense of her best friend.

Once it opened and the public arrived, the fete was reasonably successful and Helena found she enjoyed manning the bookstall. There were plenty of people coming by for a chat as they browsed through the books. She didn't make many sales, but at least some of the stock was gone and a bit of money had been raised for cancer research. She wasn't entirely sure what happened to the leftover items—there was enough to hold another fair without there needing to be any more donations. The cake stall was the only one that had sold everything. It was probably for the best; it wasn't as though cakes would last for another event. Fortunately, she had purchased a few home-made cakes and biscuits before the fair opened. As the last few members of the public drifted away, Helena handed her ice-cream tub full of money over to Bill to be counted up. It had a satisfying weight to it, and she was happy to think she hadn't been completely wasting her time.

"It seems to have gone well," she said, smiling.

"Yes, quite a good turn out," Bill replied. "Of course, the cake stall and sausage sizzle is where we take most of the money, but people like to have the other stalls to look around."

"What do you want me to do with all of the leftover books?"

She gestured toward her table and Bill looked at the books still spread across her stall.

"Pack them back into the boxes. Someone from the pony club will pick them up at five."

"The pony club? What do they want them for?" Helena asked, confused. A pony club seemed like the last place a few boxes of second-hand books would be wanted.

"They've got a fun day and fair coming up in a few weeks. They're going to take all of our unsold things. It happens with all the local groups. We got half of this stuff from the Playcentre after their recent garage sale."

"Doesn't everyone notice it's the same things, going from one place to the next?" Helena asked, quite surprised that each local group just seemed to share their stock from one event to the next. Presumably never expected to reduce the amount of it too much, especially when they no doubt had new donations to add each time.

"Not usually. Different people go to each event and it's surprising what people can miss at one place, but decide they want at another. It saves a trip to the tip or a charity shop. These days, they're not usually keen to come out and collect leftovers and it makes collecting items for the next fair easier if you've already got some stock from another event to use. There's always lots leftover at the end of these things. More than we'd know what to do with if there wasn't someone willing to take it over."

Helena began to pile things into the boxes, ready to be collected. She started putting them in some kind of order, keeping the books in theme and type. She was probably wasting her time she realized, as the next person to put them out for sale would probably have a different idea about how they should be organized. Giving up, she stacked them in the boxes in the best order they fit, managing to fit the lids back on was probably more helpful.

"Well, I'm all done, so I'll be off then," Cathy called as she walked out of the hall. With all of her cakes sold, there remained little for her to do at the end of the fair. Helena couldn't help but wonder if this was another of the reasons she preferred to sell cakes to second-hand items.

"Bye," Helena called back.

Bill wandered back over to Helena as she finished packing the boxes and stacked them to one side ready for collection.

"Thanks for all of your help, Helena, I haven't got the final amount yet, but I think we've made quite a healthy donation for the charity."

"Oh good. I'm glad it went well," she said, brushing her hands off as she stood up.

"Yes, I don't know what was wrong with Cathy earlier. She is usually quite keen to stick around and find out how we've done. She seemed a bit off today though, a bit short with me when I took her money," Bill said.

Helena felt a prickle of discomfort when she considered why Cathy was probably in this mood, remembering their earlier conversation.

"Ah," she said, "that might be my fault. I was

talking about my visit to John the other day and I mentioned his sister Jessie. Cathy seemed to get very upset when I brought her up."

"I see, yes, she was never her number one fan. Of course, it didn't help that her husband, Frank, was one of Jessie's biggest fans." He raised his eyebrows and gave her a significant look that implied there had been something between Cathy's late husband and Jessie.

"I did wonder. She seemed a little too adamant he hadn't liked her at all. It seemed to be a strange reaction."

"Yes, there were quite a few men who lost their heads over her. She was a pretty young thing, though, and I think a lot of them thought they stood a chance with her. Silly old fools, of course, they never did."

Bill paused, seemingly lost in his memories.

"Were you one of her admirers then?" Helena asked with a grin.

"Me?" Bill laughed. "Not really. She was nice enough, but my wife was ill at the time. I was far too busy taking care of her without running around after a young thing like that. She was always very kind to me though, always a smile and a kind word."

"You don't know where she went?" Helena asked, wondering if Bill could shed some more light on the mystery.

"Jessie? No. She just vanished one day. I couldn't tell you exactly when, to be honest. She just suddenly wasn't around as much. As I say, Jan, my wife, was sick at the time. She would have passed away around then, I think, so it wasn't the most important thing on my mind."

Helena nodded, thinking about what he'd said. If

his wife had been sick back then and died not long after, then he probably wouldn't be much help in remembering if Jessie had ever said anything about where she was going or why. He was quite a bit older than Jessie and it was unlikely he knew her well or anything about her, other than just seeing her around in the community.

"No, I can understand that. It just seemed odd she went and vanished like that," Helena said.

Bill nodded in a distracted way before going back to tidying up one of the other stalls. Helena hoped she hadn't upset him, reminding him of when his wife had died. She seemed to have a talent for stirring up unpleasant memories for people today. Looking around at the boxes she had packed, everything seemed ready to go. The fair had surprisingly taken it out of her and she was ready for a sit down at home. Gathering up her jacket and bag, she headed toward the door.

"I'll be off then unless you need me for anything else?" she called out to Bill.

"No, that's all. Thanks for all your help. Can I give you a call about the next meeting?" Bill said.

"Yes, that's fine. I should be free. See you soon."

"Bye, dear, and thanks again."

Just as she was about to step outside the hall, Bill called out to her again.

"Oh, Helena, I'm just wondering. What was it that made you start asking questions about Jessie?"

Helena turned back toward him.

"Well, nothing really. There was a photo in John's things, and I just wondered who she was and what happened to her."

Bill nodded.

"She was no one really," he said. "No one of any interest, anyway, and I don't think she's that missed now she's gone."

Helena stepped out of the hall. Jessie might not be around here anymore, but she certainly wasn't no one. She didn't like the idea of anyone being so easily dismissed. But someone who was no one wouldn't cause such a reaction among people when her name came up. Especially after all this time.

Chapter 10

As Helena got into her car, she noticed the local garage was still open. She was surprised to see it still open, as it usually closed earlier on the weekends. She usually waited until her gas tank was almost empty before filling up. However, this seemed like a good opportunity to stop by and inquire if anyone at the garage might remember Murray.

Helena drove onto the forecourt and pumped twenty dollars' worth of petrol into the car. Often, someone would come out and serve you. Helena liked this old-fashioned approach, rather than the self-service most places offered these days. She walked into the little shop where you could purchase magazines, local milk and honey and chocolate bars, along with a rather eclectic array of hardware items. Standing behind the counter was one of the men who worked in the garage itself as a mechanic usually, rather than one of the staff members who worked behind the counter usually selling petrol. It must have been getting close to closing time, with fewer staff on duty than there were during the week.

"Pump four? Twenty dollars please," he said as Helena reached the counter.

"Thanks."

Helena slid her bank card into the machine and tapped in the PIN. After it cleared, she glanced up at the man. He was a little younger than her, in his forties perhaps, although it wasn't always easy to tell with someone who had probably spent much of his working life outdoors. He might have been a little too young to have worked when Murray was still here, but there was a chance he knew something of him or had heard one of his colleagues mentioning him before. He'd been in the business for some time. Helena noticed as she took her receipt that his hands were clean, but with an ingrained dirty greasiness, which no doubt came from years of working with cars and engines. He looked friendly enough and Helena decided he was as good a person to ask as any.

"I was just wondering," she said, "were you here when someone called Murray worked here?"

"Murray? Murray who?" he replied with a frown. Helena got the distinct impression he might be there in body, but his mind was already making the journey back home or down to one of the local pubs.

"I'm not sure, sorry. It would have been quite a while ago now though, nearly thirty years I think. Apparently, he used to work here?"

He paused, considering. Helena wondered what she might say to him when he asked why she wanted to know, particularly when she didn't know much about the man she was asking about. Perhaps it would have been a good idea to have planned this a little better.

"Oh, do you mean Murray MacPherson? He used to work here years ago. Would have been in the late eighties, early nineties though, something like that I think."

"That could be him. It would have been about that long ago. I don't suppose you know what happened to him?" Helena felt a spark of excitement—she was on the right track. '

"It's a bit before my time. Dad was still working here then; he knew him quite well. He trained him as an apprentice before he took me on. Murray did some of the basics with me when I was still a kid and liked to come in and help out, but he left before I started working here properly and that was in ninety-two."

He paused, remembering. Helena held her breath, wondering if he'd be able to tell her anything else that might be of use. She could look Murray up online, now she had a surname, but anything else might help to narrow down the search.

"He lives in Cromwell now I heard. His uncle owned the mechanic shop there and he moved back to take it over once he was fully trained. I think he wanted his own place and knew I'd be taking this on from Dad eventually. Yeah, MacPherson's it's called," he said with a nod.

"Oh, right, thanks. That's really helpful, thank you." Helena slid her bank card back into her wallet and turned to leave. She hoped she could get out of there before he asked why she wanted to know, still having not managed to think up a plausible excuse for her interest in this old employee.

"What were you wanting to know about him for?" he asked.

She sighed and turned back at the man. "Someone mentioned him the other day, or his girlfriend at the time rather. I just wondered if he knew anything about what had happened to her," she said, attempting to be vague and hoping he wouldn't push for more information.

He suddenly frowned, the open and friendly expression he'd had completely gone at once, almost as though shutters had come down. Yet another person who seemed less than thrilled by the infamous Jessie it would seem. Perhaps it would be best to let this go and stop asking questions about someone who was not very well-liked. Who would have thought asking about some young woman who hadn't lived in the area for thirty years would cause such strong reactions?

"I'd forgotten about her. Caused him a lot of trouble as I remember. What was her name, Jackie or Janet or something." He shook his head as though to clear it. "I don't think he'd know much about her to be honest. Or want to for that matter."

"No?"

"No. They split up before he left. He was quite cut up about it. I remember Dad telling him she wasn't worth it and to go home and come back with his mind on the job again when it happened. Yeah, Dad said to me women are often more trouble than they're worth and I'd learn that when I was older." He laughed, the previous discomfort seemingly forgotten. "Not that I took any notice—that's one you have to learn for yourself the hard way of course."

"Well, thanks anyway, it wasn't important, I just thought I'd ask in case you could remember anything."

"Probably best left alone. He's got a wife and family now, last I heard, and no one wants things stirred up about a girlfriend from thirty-odd years ago, do they?"

"No, I suppose not. Bye, then, and thanks."

****

When she arrived back home, Helena had the

house to herself. Dave had mentioned he was going out for a bike ride while she was out at the fair and he hadn't returned home again yet. Pouring herself a glass of wine, she opened up her computer. Surely it wouldn't hurt if she just had a quick look to see if it was possible to track down this Murray MacPherson. Now she had his name, it wasn't long before she'd managed to find him with a quick online search. He, at least, had a social media profile, although he didn't seem particularly active on it. Someone called Amy MacPherson had tagged him in some photos that weren't set as private. His wife, perhaps? She certainly didn't look as though she could be Jessie.

Even with the passage of thirty years or so, Helena wasn't convinced someone could have changed so much. This must be a different woman. The theory perhaps Jessie had left with him seemed to be out of the window. Unless, of course, she had left with him and then gone on elsewhere without him after the relationship had run its course. They had both been quite young at the time and relationships at that age often didn't last the distance. Either idea did nothing to explain why she had never returned to the area again or been to see her brother, even for a visit.

She soon tracked down the address for Murray's garage, along with his telephone number. It was listed on a few service and review sites and seemed to be the main mechanical garage for the whole Cromwell area, no doubt spending most of its time servicing farm vehicles in that area. Now the only question was whether to try to call him about Jessie or not. So far, people had not been very forthcoming when talking about her. The girl seemed to still be able to upset many of the locals, even after all this time. If Murray had been cut up over their break-up, he certainly might not appreciate talking about Jessie now. Especially as he now had a wife, family, and life that had nothing to do with an old girlfriend. Helena hesitated, holding the phone in one hand, trying to decide whether to dial the number or not.

Nothing ventured, nothing gained, she quickly dialed the number before she could change her mind. She half expected there to be no answer on a Saturday afternoon at the garage, but someone picked up on the second ring.

"MacPherson Motors, Murray speaking," said a male voice.

"Oh, hi. I'm sorry to bother you, but I was wondering if you could help me with something," Helena said. "I'm trying to track down Jessie Andrews from Port Chalmers and I understand you might have known her?"

There was silence for a second and then a brief bark of incredulous laughter on the end of the line as he took in what she had asked.

"I'm sorry, I know this must be a bit strange." she rushed on, hoping he wouldn't just hang up without saying anything else.

"No, it's just that's a name I haven't heard for a long time. Yes, I knew Jessie, but I haven't heard anything of her since I left Port myself, that was years ago. Not sure I can help you find out anything about her now."

"No, I realize and I'm sorry for calling. It's just no one seems to know what happened to her after she left, and I'd heard you were close, and I thought there was at least a chance that maybe you knew something."

There was silence again for a second and Helena wasn't sure if Murray was going to continue to talk to her.

"Who is this?" he asked, suspicion lacing his words.

"Sorry, I should have said. My name is Helena and I live near Port. I know her brother John and he mentioned no one knew where she'd gone. So, I was trying to find out for him, to see if I could help track her down or find out what had happened to her. I'm sorry this is a bit out of the blue, but I just thought it was worth a chance, speaking to someone who used to know her back then."

"John doesn't know where she is? Well, that surprises me, they were close. As I say, though, I haven't seen her since before I left. We split up about then and it was pretty obvious there was no point trying to stay in touch even if I had known where she went."

His surprise that John didn't know where Jessie disappeared to seemed genuine. There was still a chance he might have known why she had left, or at least have been able to give a hint as to why it might have happened.

"I'm sorry to bring this all up again, I just thought that you might remember something that could help me track her down. She might have mentioned where she might go to or something?"

"No, I'm sorry." He sighed. "I was crazy about her at one point. She'd convinced me to leave, move with her to Australia, and forget all about coming back here to take on my uncle's garage business. She wanted to get away and I'd tried convincing her we could move out here, but it wasn't far enough or exotic enough for Jessie. She had big dreams. She'd arranged to meet me in town. The plan was to drive up to Christchurch, sell the car, and then get a flight to Australia. But she never turned up. I sat and waited in my car for hours, but she never came. I called her house and John said her stuff had gone. I don't know, she must have changed her mind about going with me and gone off on her own."

It was difficult over the phone, but as far as she could tell, he sounded truthful. 'Had she carried out her own plan? Perhaps she really had just left without him.

"You didn't hear from her again after that?" Helena asked.

"No. I thought she was just mad at me for some reason. Our relationship was a bit volatile at the best of times, and when she never made any attempt to make up or get back in touch, I thought it was pretty obvious things were finally over between us. We'd had a bit of a row, see. I didn't like how friendly she was with some of those creepy old men."

"Creepy old men? Who were they?" Helena asked.

"I don't suppose they were that old, in their forties maybe, seemed old to me at the time. Bill what's his name and Frank something from the local church. They were always all over her like a rash. She loved the attention, but I didn't like how they behaved, as though she belonged to them. After the row we had, I just thought she'd had enough of me and decided to go off on her own.

"I did think she might decide to get back in touch once she'd calmed down, but she never did. I pined over her for a while and then got on with it. Ended up moving back here and getting on with my own life."

Helena had thought there might have been something going on with Cathy's husband Frank, but hearing Bill's name in connection with Jessie was completely unexpected. Perhaps Murray was mistaken about that though, if Bill's wife had been ill, then he might not have had the time to get involved with Jessie. It sounded as though Murray had been jealous, but it didn't necessarily mean there was any foundation to his fears.

"Bill as well as Frank? I didn't realize that he had known her that well."

"He was the worst one for it, didn't seem to care that she was almost young enough to be his daughter. He was all over her. She wasn't interested or anything like that, but Jessie just loved attention. She got a kick out of leading them on a bit."

"I see, well thank you, Murray. I'm sorry I brought it up for you again."

"No worries. I moved on years ago. in all honesty, I haven't even thought about her in a long, long time. Good luck with finding her."

"Thanks, bye." Helena hung up and stood for a few minutes thinking about the conversation.

Jessie hadn't wanted to remain in Port Chalmers. Her intended plan was to leave with Murray but hadn't followed through. From the little Helena had learned about Jessie so far, she seemed like the kind of person who liked to get her own way. Men chasing after her was not something Jessie frowned upon, and perhaps Murray arguing with her had been enough for her to decide to just go off on her own. Or something happened that made her decide she didn't need someone else with her after all. She might even have met someone that she thought was a better choice than Murray.

If she'd been close to her brother as Murray had suggested, it seemed strange she hadn't stayed in touch with him over the years, other than the postcards. But perhaps there had been some kind of fall out there too. The more Helena thought about it, the more likely it seemed. It would also explain why John hadn't spent any time himself trying to track Jessie down. Maybe he'd said something that had erupted into an argument, and she'd stormed off and left forever. From what she'd heard from the people who had known her, Jessie wasn't one to keep her feelings to herself. She apparently upset people all over the place. Perhaps she'd just decided a clean break was the best option.

Chapter 11

Some things are better just left alone. Or at least that was what Helena kept telling herself. For some reason, it was impossible to take her own advice. Perhaps it would be better to forget all about Jessie. Having started down this path, she couldn't fathom the idea of abandoning it. There had to be something in this and the body—something to do with Jessie. Or maybe not. Either way, an unidentified woman had lain buried for years and a girl had left, never to return at around the same time. Helena couldn't let it go until she had answers about Jessie's whereabouts or confirmed the body wasn't connected to her.

The next morning was a Sunday and with few other plans for the day, Helena decided another trip to Pūrākaunui to visit John again was a good idea. Her previous visit had been friendly enough and surely it wouldn't hurt to go back for a second time. He'd even invited her to pop in again if she had the chance. If there was anyone who could help her get to the bottom of what had happened to Jessie, then her brother seemed to be the obvious choice.

She grabbed a bag with some baking she'd bought at the fair the day before and headed for the door. If she'd been a little more like Cathy or Diane, then no doubt she would have whipped something up herself, but she'd never claimed to be anyone's idea of the perfect housewife. Even with her recent foray into the world of local institutions, she wasn't about to add regular home baker to her CV. Becoming more like Cathy or Diane seemed less than appealing in any case.

"I'll see you later," she called to David on her way out. "I'm heading over to John's to see if he'll tell me a bit more about his sister."

"Is that a good idea? He might not appreciate more questions about something that happened so long ago. Do you think you should be stirring everything up?"

David appeared in the doorway from the bedroom, scratching his belly. He wasn't looking as bright and awake as Helena, still dressed in pyjama bottoms, a t-shirt, and well-worn slippers. He ran a hand through his receding gray hair and stretched.

"I'm just going to ask a couple of things. If he's not keen, I'll leave it. He told me to pop in again soon and I'm sure he'd like some of this baking I got from the fair."

"I thought I was going to get to eat that," he said, pulling a mock disappointed face.

She laughed. "I'm only thinking of you. If it's here you'll eat it and then complain you shouldn't have done. I'm saving you those extra hours you'd have to put in on the bike."

He grinned at her. "Just be careful, okay?"

"I will be, don't worry. I don't want to cause trouble, just find out what happened." She kissed his cheek before heading to the door. "I'll see you later."

"See you later," he said with a yawn, before heading back inside the bedroom with another stretch.

****

It was a beautiful winter's day, as Helena headed

out of Port Chalmers and up toward Pūrākaunui and Long Beach. The sun had finally broken through the cloud cover and lit up the sea across the harbor and out toward the horizon. The views as she climbed up above Port were breathtaking and Helena smiled as she drove to John's farm. 'No matter how many times she took in this scenery, it always lifted her spirits with gratitude, thankful for living in such a stunning part of the world. The light seemed different at this time of day. The sun might be fully out, but somehow the colors were softer, less bright than in the height of summer. It made the landscape dramatic and almost unreal. Compared to her previous visit, when the sky had been dark and rain threatened, the place looked completely transformed. On a day like today, it felt like nothing bad could ever happen, and that it never had.

John opened the door as Helena walked up the path to his house.

"I thought I saw your car. Can't keep away?" he said with a chuckle as he held open the door for her.

"Something like that. I thought you might like some of the baking from the fair yesterday. There are some scones and a couple of cupcakes, I think." She held up the carrier bag to show him with a grin.

"Lovely. I'll get the jug on, and we can have a couple with a cup of tea, if you like. It's a while since I've had any home baking. I don't bother making anything since it's just me."

She followed him into the cozy living room and passed the bag over to him.

"I can't take any credit for these. I'm not much of a baker myself, to be honest. It would have been one of the others, Cathy or Diane or someone else, maybe."

"In for a treat then, it's been a while, but I remember them both being first-class cake bakers." he said as he peered into the contents of the bag.'

Helena followed him into the kitchen, where he started to make a pot of tea. She leaned against one of the work surfaces that stretched around two edges of the tidy room. The kitchen was like the rest of the house, clean, tidy, but dated. The kitchen cupboards and work surfaces looked as though they had been in the house since it was built in the 1970s. They did their job, but the style showed their age. Parts of the Formica work surface were worn and faded with use. Everything was functional but lacking the homely touch a woman often brought. Helena looked at John. He was Jessie's older brother, but even so, he could only be in his fifties at the very oldest, somewhere around her own age. Somehow, though, he seemed to be much older than that. Perhaps it was living out here on his own, being cut off from the rest of the local population. Whatever it was, something had aged him beyond his years.

"Was Bill happy with the history stuff?" he asked as he made the tea.

"Yes, I think so. I didn't get a chance to ask when I gave it to him at the fair. I had a quick look through it too. It was quite interesting. I think saw a photo of your sister in there?"

"Yes, outside the pub? That's her. She was quite into local history. It always made me laugh because she was so keen to get away from here, but didn't mind learning about what it used to be like."

"She didn't want to stick around then?" Helena asked.

"No, that's part of the reason I wasn't surprised she

left. She loved it here when we were kids, both here at the farm and down in town, but once she hit the teenage years, she was desperate to spread her wings. She had this theory that people never left. Even those who went overseas or up north, always end up moving back here. She's not far wrong. Most people seem to come back here eventually."

"I'm guessing Jessie didn't plan to be like that then? She never had any plans to come back once she left."

They walked into the lounge and sat on the armchairs as they continued their conversation. John had put the scones and cakes onto a plate and held them out for Helena to select one.

"No, she was determined once she left, that would be it, she wouldn't come back. I don't know though. She said that, but I still expected her to return, even if it was just for a visit, eventually."

"But she never has?" Helena bit into the cupcake she'd selected. As she savored the delicious flavor, she couldn't help but think how grateful it was that her baking attempts weren't going to be measured against this masterpiece—she'd never be able to come anywhere near close.

"No, never, and now I don't even get the postcards. I don't know why she stopped sending them, or what happened to her."

They sat in silence for a few minutes, eating and drinking. Helena couldn't help but wonder why John hadn't done more to track down his sister. Even if he hadn't been worried, to begin with, surely after all this time you'd have started to wonder where she was and worry about what had happened to her. Especially if they had been as close as other people seemed to have suggested. John spoke again, almost as though he had been able to hear what she'd been thinking.

"I don't know…I've always just expected her to walk through the door, but the longer time has gone on, it just hasn't happened. I wouldn't know where to start looking for her now."

"You've no idea at all where she could have gone to?"

He shook his head.

"I wouldn't have a clue where to start, to be honest. The postcards were from Australia, but never from the same place. She seemed to travel around all the time, so she could be anywhere. She may not have even been living over there, just visiting once a year when she sent the card."

Helena looked over to the postcards stacked on the mantelpiece and walked over to have a closer look. Flipping them over, she looked at the different postmarks. John was right—no two consecutive postcards were from the same place. It was as though she had been trying to throw everyone off the scent, or if she were sending them when travelling around Australia. They were sent at roughly the same time each year, between mid-October and early December. There was even one from Auckland, from a few years ago but again dated at the end of October. Then, suddenly, they stopped; no cards dated later than about five years ago.

"Is it her writing?" Helena asked.

Bill frowned and held his hand out for one of the cards. He studied it closely.

"I'd never thought about that," he said. "The first one was a month or so after she left, and we had no reason to think it wasn't her sending it. No, it must be her writing. She always wrote her name like that, with the heart over the I, rather than a dot." He held the card out, pointing at the name at the bottom. "I didn't see her writing very often before she left, neither did Dad, to be honest, but I remember her signing her name like that."

Helena took the card from him and looked at the signature. Sure enough, there was a little heart over the top of the I. Something stirred uneasily at the back of her mind as she looked at the card, something she couldn't quite put her finger on. She looked at the date.

"Did she always sign off like this? I mean, I can see a young girl doing it. She was what, eighteen or nineteen when she left?"

"Just after her nineteenth birthday, yes," John confirmed, looking at the card over Helena's shoulder.

"But I would have thought a woman in her mid-thirties, as she would have been when this one had been sent, might have grown out of that." Helena held up another, more recent card. The name on it was the same as it had been on the earlier cards. Almost as though it was printed, although it was clearly written in pen. It looked carefully copied, rather than the flowing, organic way most people scribbled their names. Each of the names was exactly the same, with no slight differences or changes over time on any of them.

"I don't know. Jessie was one of a kind. Maybe she never did grow up properly, that wouldn't surprise me. I don't know. Hadn't thought about it before."

Helena returned the cards to the mantelpiece, her mind churning as she thought about it all. Had Jessie sent the cards each year? If she hadn't sent them, then who on earth would have had the motivation to keep it up for so long and how did they manage to send them from Australia? Then there was the question of why they had stopped. It all seemed very odd, and Helena was sure she would have the answers to all of her questions if she could answer those she had about the postcards.

"I don't suppose I could take a couple of the cards with me?" she asked.

"What for?"

"Well, I just thought it might be worth showing them to the police, seeing what they think about the cards if they are really from her."

John leaped up, an angry frown etched on his face.

"The police?! Why would they be interested? What exactly are you suggesting? That I've somehow faked cards from my sister somehow? What for?"

For a moment, Helena got a small glimpse of the anger that no doubt ran in John's family. She had heard his father was known for his temper and it seemed John had inherited some of it himself.

"No, no, that's not what I meant," she said quickly. "I just wondered if someone else could have written them. I'm sorry, it was a silly thought, forget it."

John didn't look immediately convinced, but after a moment he relaxed somewhat and the anger seemed to be forgotten. She hadn't meant to upset him by asking, but it was clear the cards were important to him. She stayed for a little longer. Chatting to him about the fair and people she knew that he might also know. These days, he clearly rarely got into Port Chalmers itself, but at one time he must have been there a lot. He knew many of the people who were still around in the community and shared a few amusing anecdotes about his younger years.

It was an enjoyable visit, but all the time she was there, her mind was racing. The more she found out about Jessie, the more convinced she was that the girl was somehow connected to the body she had found. It also seemed the more she looked into it, the more people that seemed to be connected to her in some way. She left John's house after they had finished the coffee and cakes and sat in the car for a few moments thinking it all through. It was about time she spoke to the police again. If no one knew Jessie was missing, if she hadn't been reported as missing to the authorities, then it was unlikely they would be looking to see if she could be connected to the body. Someone had to consider the possibility that Jessie was somehow involved in the mystery of the dead body or perhaps even the dead girl herself.

Chapter 12

The police station was much quieter than the last time Helena had been there. As she approached the building, she noticed there were no longer many cars parked outside, almost deserted quality. At first, Helena worried the station might not be open. Taking a second, closer look at the building, she was relieved to see the main door was ajar, indicating somebody was still inside.

Helena climbed out of the car and walked up the steps, clutching the photo of Jessie in front of the pub she had found in the local history folder. She had considered asking John for more photos but knew it was wrong to do so until she could be sure of her suspicions. Especially after his reaction when she had asked for the postcards. She didn't want to draw attention to her suspicions until the police had the chance to look into them. No doubt it would be down to the police in any case, should they need more photos.

There was no one behind the counter. Looking around for signs of life, she rang the bell on the counter and waited for someone to come and deal with her.

****

Sarah walked through to the main counter. She hadn't been expecting anyone this late on a Sunday and had been tidying things away in the back, before heading off home herself. As a general rule, the police station usually closed over the weekend. Instead, Sarah usually spent her on-duty days out in the community talking to people, leaving contact details should anyone need to reach her. As the station wasn't manned all the time, there was also a telephone set into a little cabinet on the front door which connected directly with the main station back in Dunedin. Since the body had been discovered, they decided to increase police visibility and rostered extra shifts, with additional officers coming from Dunedin to help Sarah cover the area. The police station was to be opened seven days a week, at least for the time being, while the community came to terms with what had happened and in case anyone had any information they wanted to share with the police. The sooner things were back to normal and quieter again, the better.

"Oh, hello. Helena isn't it?" she said with a little bit of surprise, seeing Helena standing waiting for her. "What can I do to help you?"

"I'm sorry to bother you. I've just been thinking a lot about the body I found. There were just a few things I wanted to ask, or explain, or I don't know, talk to you about, I suppose." Helena's words tumbled out in a rush.

"Okay." Sarah nodded encouragingly. "Would you like to come through?"

Sarah lifted the counter for Helena to follow her to the back office. Compared to the last visit, this time there was no sound from the other rooms, other than the two of them walking into the echoing room. The other detectives and members of the investigation who had filled the space before had left, returning to their comfortable desks at the Dunedin Station.

"Has everyone left?" Helena asked with surprise, looking around.

"Yes, they've all gone back to town now. Most of the work can be done from there and they've got the right kind of equipment and technology they need for modern crime-fighting."

Sarah said the last bit with a grimace, acknowledging the management speak as a little embarrassing and unnecessary.

"Oh, I thought maybe it meant they'd solved it all or something." Helena's little laugh gave away her embarrassment.

"No, not yet. Being as it's thirty years since it happened, it will take some time. It might never actually be solved, of course, but either way, they just didn't need to be here anymore. Anyway, there was something you wanted to talk about?" Sarah prompted. She indicated the table, inviting Helena to take a seat, while picking up a pad and pen, ready to note down anything of importance Helena had to share.

"Look, this might be nothing, but I had a thought about who the body might be. That is, assuming she hasn't been identified as yet?" Helena asked.

Sarah shook her head. "No firm identification, no, but they are working on several leads." This was the standard response, suggesting to the general public that the police were completely in the dark about the identity of the body. This not knowing didn't help to foster confidence in the force, or at least that was what the 'powers that be' believed. They were always very hot on making sure their police officers presented a united and competent front to the public, even when they were completely in the dark. Sarah privately had often felt it was possibly better to be honest, encouraging people to come to them with extra information they might otherwise think was no longer needed. But she was just a lowly constable in a local police station, what did she know about these things? She kept out of the politics of the main Dunedin station as much as possible. If she didn't bother them, then hopefully they wouldn't bother her either.

"Well, this might be nothing, but there's this girl, well—woman, who went missing around here about thirty years ago. She was about nineteen, I think," Helena said. There was an urgency to the way she spoke, as if she felt the need to rush her words out, yet too scared to tell the police what she had found.

Sarah looked at her with surprise. This wasn't what she had been expecting. She knew all of the local missing person records had been investigated in great detail and the idea there might be someone who not only matched the age of the victim but had also gone missing around the same time she had been murdered seemed improbable and surprising.

"I don't remember any mention of someone of that age being on the missing person register for that period. Certainly not local to here, anyway." Sarah frowned as she recalled the details of the case. Could they have missed someone?

"No, well, you see, that's the thing. She is missing, but she isn't officially missing. No one has seen her since then. Her family thought she'd left for Australia, but I'm not so sure she did." Again, Helena's words rushed out.

"But they didn't try and find her or report she was missing?" Sarah said skeptically. It didn't sound very likely.

"No, you see, she, or rather someone, has been sending postcards once a year from different parts of Australia, but I don't know if they are actually from her. Here." Helena pulled out a small bundle of cards and handed them over. "The date on this one is a couple of years after she left, see? But this one is one of the last ones, from about eight years ago. In all that time, she hasn't changed the way she's written her name. Not even slightly. It's almost as though it's printed or, which I think is more likely, copied very carefully. I don't know, and I might be reading far more into this than is there, but I just think a grown woman would have changed it slightly over time."

Sarah looked the cards over, flipping each one to see where they were sent from and if there was any further information on them. They were generic tourist postcards, with tourist attractions from the areas of Australia they came from. The message on both was similar. Telling her family that all was good, and she was happy, and, in both cases, it was signed simply Jessie. The signature was almost identical, more so even than you would expect from the same person writing their name. Not that Sarah was an expert, it would take some kind of handwriting analysis to confirm there was something odd about the cards. But she could see what Helena was getting at. Even the message itself didn't vary much between the cards.

"Well, there's not a lot here to go on. Are there more of these cards? And you say her family haven't heard anything else in all that time?" Sarah frowned, looking at the postcards. It was certainly a little unusual. She would have had concerns about this Jessie had her disappearance been reported ordinarily, but with the added question of the body of a missing girl from around the same period, she couldn't help but wonder if this was the missing clue they had been looking for.

"No, not a thing. The cards stopped about five years ago and there's been nothing since then. Before that, there had been one a year since she left. I don't know, it might be nothing, but I did think that if she really is missing, but no one knew that she was…well, then that might be important? Especially as she left at around the time you mentioned the body was buried there." Helena looked at Sarah hopefully.

"Hmm, possibly. It's certainly worth our looking into. But we don't know exactly when this body was buried there. It might have been anytime in a period about thirty years ago. It could just be a coincidence." Even as she spoke, Sarah wasn't sure she believed that. "The cards are addressed to John Andrews, she's his…?"

"Sister, younger sister. John lives out at Pūrākaunui, the same address that's on the cards there. He's been in the same house for years."

"I know of John, but I didn't know he had any family, to be honest. I'll pass this information on, thank you."

Helena smiled, looking as though a weight had been lifted off her shoulders.

"Thanks for this, Helena," Sarah said. "I'd strongly advise you leave things to us now, though. I know you've got a personal interest in this, having found the body, but it's best to not get too involved yourself."

"Yes, I know, I'm sorry. I just couldn't stop

thinking about her and then when I met John and he told me about his sister, I couldn't help but wonder if there was something there."

Sarah nodded, understanding that feeling, but it was different for her. She was a policewoman, and it was her job to look into things like this. The last thing they needed was every busybody in the area poking their nose into active investigations, no matter how well-meaning the person was.

They stood and made their way back through to the front of the police station. Helena walked through the gap in the counter and to the front door with Sarah following behind, turning off lights as she went.

"That's understandable. But I think you might be better off forgetting about it for now and perhaps looking into that counseling I mentioned?" Sarah said.

"Yes, yes, I will, thank you."

"See you soon, and thanks again," Sarah said, closing the door behind Helena as she stepped out of the station and headed back to her car. Sarah returned to the counter and picked up the telephone. She would call the team working on the case straight away. She suspected she wasn't going to be relaxing at home that evening for quite some time yet.

Chapter 13

The next few days were relatively quiet for Helena. After the excitement of the fair and learning about Jessie, nothing much seemed to happen. On Thursday, there was a meeting for those who had been involved with the recent fair. Helena had decided to attend, keeping up for the time being with her newfound community spirit. She might as well make the most of it while it lasted. There was a small part of her that was keen for some local gossip too. She wanted to know if there had been any whispers about Jessie being the missing body, or if there had been any other developments. The police may not have announced anything officially as yet, but if there was any news to be heard, it wouldn't be long before everyone knew all about it in a small community like this.

They again held the meeting in the pioneer hall. Bill, Cathy, and Diane were already there when she arrived, sitting around the table in the center of the room. Bill was at the head and sat perusing the papers he had spread around him. Cathy and Diane sat on either side, quietly watching him while they waited for the meeting to begin. For some reason, Helena couldn't help feeling she was intruding somehow, as though she had walked into a meeting that outsiders were not welcome at. Perhaps it was just this time she had arrived after everyone else. Bill looked up, and seeing her, smiled.

"Ah, Helena, I was beginning to wonder if you'd be joining us. Grab a seat," he said, gesturing to the other end of the table.

"Sorry, am I late? I didn't realize." She smiled at the three of them sitting there, and then turned toward Cathy and Diane. "Hi."

They nodded back at her. Diane had brought some knitting along with her and seemed engrossed in working on it with her needles flying as she peered at a printed pattern. Helena didn't know what had happened, but for some reason, they all seemed to be less pleased to see her than they had been on previous occasions. Even Bill, who had always been much more welcoming than the two women, seemed to be reserved. He had smiled, but there didn't seem to be much warmth or genuine welcome behind it. It was as though he didn't know what to say to Helena or that he had rethought the idea of having new blood to help out with the group.

"No, you're not late," he said briskly. "We were just here a bit early."

"Is everything all right?" Helena asked, looking around at them nervously.

Again, it was Bill who spoke. "Yes, I think everyone is a little out of sorts with all this bother over the body that was found." Although she was fairly certain everyone now knew it was her who had discovered the body, he spoke as though it was something that had happened independently, and she had no involvement in it. Perhaps becoming part of the community was a little more complicated than just living here and attending the odd meeting.

"Oh? I thought that had all blown over now. Has something new happened?" Helena held her breath waiting to hear the answer.

"Yes, there's been a few questions asked about Jessie Andrews," Cathy said, suddenly and finally breaking her silence. "I know you can't help having found the body, but I think some of us could have done without being reminded about that little harlot."

Helena's eyebrows shot up, realizing people might not have been too happy with Jessie in the past. Cathy's comments the last time they had spoken about her had made that clear, but her reaction now was aggressive. Helena felt herself mentally, if not physically, recoil away from Cathy's anger. She glanced across at Diane, remembering what she had told her about Cathy and Jessie. Diane avoided eye contact, giving all of her attention to the knitting she was doing. It was clear she had no intention of being drawn into anything this time.

"Oh, I'm sorry. I know I mentioned her the other day, but I didn't mean to cause anyone any problems." Helena paused for a second, wondering how to break the tension in the room, but determined to uncover the answers she desperately sought. "Does this mean they think there might be some connection between the body and this Jessie then?"

Diane and Cathy looked at one another for a moment. It was a look full of meaning, but not meaning she could easily read. Although Helena had been desperate to find out who the body was and how, if at all, Jessie fitted into the story, she suddenly felt uncomfortable and almost wished she hadn't got involved in this. Coming to this meeting seemed to have been a mistake. Finally, Diane answered her.

"I don't think they know as yet. But her name has been cropping up over the last few days. The police have been asking questions, talking to people who knew her or who were around then. People have wanted to know about Bill and Frank, Cathy's husband, that is, and their relationship with her."

"There wasn't a relationship!" Cathy spat out, glaring at Diane. Her anger, thankfully, was now directed away from Helena.

"I don't think that's what Diane meant," Bill said placatingly. "I didn't have a relationship with the girl either. They were just trying to establish how we all knew her."

"Yes, yes," Diane said quickly. "I wasn't suggesting there was anything wrong. On Frank and Bill's part. at least. We all know what *she* could be like."

An awkward silence descended over the group again. Helena looked at Bill and couldn't help but notice his expression had darkened. Somehow, she wasn't convinced he shared the women's view of Jessie entirely. Jessie must have been a woman who brought out a protective streak in the men around her, at the very least. She seemed to have drawn many toward her, upsetting the women in their lives in the process. He wasn't willing to defend Jessie fully with Cathy and Diane in the mood they were currently in.

"There's just no need to bring all of that business up again," Cathy said. "I doubt it's her, in any case. She no doubt swanned off somewhere else to cause trouble years ago and has nothing to do with this recent discovery."

"No, you're probably right, Cathy, but they have to

look into these things. It's their job to get to the bottom of who she was and how she got there," Diane said.

"I just want them to leave things be. Disturbing the memory of my poor Frank, it's ghoulish." Cathy had folded her arms as she spoke and glared at everyone as if challenging them to disagree with her view of Jessie or how blameless 'her Frank' had been.

Helena shifted awkwardly in her seat. There was much she didn't know about Jessie and what had happened all of those years ago. Time might have passed, but there were still some open wounds where this subject was concerned. She felt responsible for bringing all of this out again. But, if there was even a chance the body could be Jessie, then she didn't see what other choice there had been. She'd had to go to Constable Hanover with the information. Perhaps she would keep that to herself, for now, because it certainly wouldn't win her any friends here. She couldn't help wondering how John was finding all of this interest in his missing sister, though.

Cathy suddenly stood up suddenly, pulling on her coat and picking up her bag as though remembering she needed to be someplace else.

"I'm sorry, but I don't think I'm in the right frame of mind for this today," she said tersely. "I'll see you next week, but I need to go home for now. Bye."

With that, she nodded her head once and walked to the door, leaving the other three sitting there looking at one another for a few moments. The silence stretched out until Bill coughed and broke the tension.

"I think we should postpone the meeting until next week, in light of, ah, recent events. I'm sure we'll all be in a much better frame of mind then, in any case," he said.

"Yes, yes, I'm sure you're right," Diane said, winding her knitting up and placing it in her bag. "I think I might go and check on Cathy. She misses Frank terribly sometimes and things like this don't help."

"Bye," Helena and Bill called after her as she hurried out of the hall after Cathy.

"I'm sorry if I've caused upset by all of this," Helena said, looking toward the now empty doorway.

"It's not your fault. You just found the body. You weren't here when there was all that trouble with Jessie, so there's no way you could have been involved in all of it or known how people felt about her. I think we should have expected something like this at some point. I'm just surprised that it's happened so long after any of us last saw her. She was a divisive character at the best of times," Bill said.

"Yes, but it's so long ago, I don't suppose anyone expected her to crop up now."

"I don't know. I've expected her to reappear every year since she left. Not quite like this, however. I just thought one day she would decide to come back home. The more time went on, the less likely it seemed, but I never quite believed she had gone forever. I'm not convinced this body has anything to do with her, in any case. I can just imagine her reappearing midway through the investigation, asking what all the fuss was about, but loving the attention. That's just the kind of thing Jessie always did."

Bill started to gather all the paperwork he'd had spread around him. Stacking it into neat and orderly piles and then clipping it back into the ring binder it had originally come from.

"She certainly seems to be able to cause trouble, even after all of this time." Helena nodded, glad that from Bill at least, the tension seemed to have dissipated a little.

"Yes, I couldn't see it at the time. I thought she was just a harmless young woman, but…" He paused, looking at Helena for a minute, but looking beyond to something that wasn't there. "She showed her true colors in the end. They always do. It was better she went."

Helena gathered the straps of her bag together and started to slip on her coat. There was a lot of bad feeling here, and she wasn't sure if she wanted to be around to push the matter further. It would be good to try and find out more, but perhaps now wasn't the time. So much for not being involved any more.

"Something happened then? Before she left?" Helena asked.

"Hmm," Bill said, breaking out of his reverie. "No, not really. It was probably the same things she'd been doing the whole time I knew her. I just hadn't seen it before. It was around the time my wife died, you know. I discovered just how heartless she was then. No compassion for the likes of me who'd been through that. No, she was only ever out for herself, and the scales fell away from my eyes very quickly, I can tell you."

"I'm sorry to hear that. Is that why you and John don't get on so well?" Helena wondered if Jessie was the cause of the dislike between the two men. Yet another relationship that had become strained because of the young woman.

"In some ways, yes. I don't think John ever woke

up to what Jessie was like. He was a bit older than her and very protective. He thought the likes of me and Cathy, who finally saw her for who she was, were awful to her. After she left, he just stopped coming into town and being part of the community. He said some things that were just not true, and I thought it was better if I kept away from him from then on. We were never very close though. He's a lot younger than I am."

"It's strange that he wasn't more concerned about her being missing, don't you think?"

Bill paused, considering the question for a moment. Helena could almost see him turning it over in his mind.

"I don't know. I think he was glad she had left, in some ways. He certainly didn't like her hanging around with some of the people around here. He never got on with that boyfriend she had from the garage. I think he was just glad she'd got away from here and from their home. Gone on to something better. I'm sure he must have heard something from her after she left, anyway. He'd have reported it if she hadn't been in touch."

"Oh, well, there were postcards, one from her each year, I think, but that was it," Helena said.

"Well, there you go, then." Bill tapped the remaining pile of papers he'd gathered together on the table to square them into a neater pile and then slapped them down into his open briefcase, as though to stamp home the point he was making. "She can't be the girl you found, and she's probably off living the high life in Australia or wherever it was she ended up. That would be Jessie all over. She never did care about anyone except herself."

"Yes, you're probably right," Helena said with a

grimace. Somehow, she couldn't quite convince herself everything was as right and neat as he claimed. "That body must belong to someone, though."

"Ah, but you forget this is a port. There are all kinds of people who've passed through. Not so many these days. There was always quite a large working girl population here, servicing the sailors from the boats and the wharfies too. Could well be one of them who came to mischief. No doubt just an accident or something has gone a bit wrong. No real mystery when it comes to it, you'll see. It wouldn't even surprise me if it's been there even longer than they think. These scientists always sound so sure of themselves, but they often make mistakes. It will be an ancient burial, in the end, you mark my words."

Bill had gathered all of his things and was walking toward the door. Helena followed him and then stepped out of the door first as he held out his arm to usher her through.

"Don't you worry about Cathy or the others. They'll have forgotten about it all by next week. Moved on to the next big bit of juicy gossip, you'll see. Now, can I interest you in a cup of tea and a slice of cake at my house?"

"No, no thank you. I need to get back home. Maybe next time, and I'm sure you're right about all of this. It will all have been forgotten about soon. I'll see you next week. Bye."

"Bye, dear, see you next time," Bill said, as he put down his briefcase and attended to locking the hall up. Helena was left feeling a little foolish about all of her ideas and worries about Jessie. Bill must have thought there was nothing more to the story than a girl running off after causing a lot of trouble. It was obvious no one who had known her thought it was odd she had just suddenly up and left.

Chapter 14

"You're back early," Helena said as she walked into the house and saw David sitting at the kitchen table. He had work spread out around him. She removed her coat and hung it on the hook by the door. They usually used this back entrance, which opened into the kitchen, rather than the more formal front door. It was closer to the driveway where they parked the car, and the kitchen had a warm and cozy feel which encouraged them to spend more time there than any of the other rooms of their house. They often sat in the kitchen during the daytime. Coming home to the welcoming, sunny room always made Helena relax and feel ready to unwind from her day.

"Hi. Yes, I canceled my last class and sent them all home. Half of them were away sick and the other half were coughing and sneezing all over the place. Didn't fancy catching it myself."

"There's a bit of it going around at the moment. It's the time of year, I suppose," Helena said as she came further into the kitchen.

"Yes, but they can keep it all to themselves! I don't want it. You know what a great patient I am."

Helena laughed as she dumped her bags on the kitchen counter.

"Coffee?" he asked.

"Sounds lovely. I could do with a cuppa and a sit-down, to be honest."

David busied himself making a hot drink, while she sank into one of the chairs at the large wooden dining table which took up most of the space in the center of the kitchen. She picked up the pile of post that was sitting there, flicked through it and returned it to the tabletop. Nothing but bills and junk mail as usual these days. The days of a personal letter and interesting communications via post seemed to have long gone.

"Rough day?" David asked.

"Yes, I thought this working less was supposed to make my life easier, not harder," she said with a wry smile.

"Ah, but you forgot the human element. That always makes a difference, no matter where you are or what you do. I'm guessing it's someone rather than something making your life difficult?"

"How did you know? Not difficult as such, just the women at the meeting today. They're not very happy about the investigating that's going into the body and that Jessie Andrews I told you about."

"Jessie Andrews? She's that farmer's sister who lives over toward Pūrākaunui, the chap you went to visit the other day?"

David finished making the drinks and brought the mugs over to the table. He placed one down in front of Helena and waited while she took her first sip. She sighed appreciatively as the hot coffee did its work, relaxing her.

"Yes, the one I was telling you about. It looks as though the police think there's something in the idea that she might be the body. I think they've been asking questions since I mentioned her to them the other day.

It seems people aren't so thrilled about them looking into it."

"Ah, well, I did warn you to be careful. What happened today, then?" David asked, frowning slightly.

"I was supposed to have another meeting to do with the fair I helped out with. Well, it was just those women I told you about, Cathy and Diane. They aren't very happy the police were investigating Jessie, well, Cathy in particular, isn't. She didn't stick around, and Bill decided to postpone the meeting until next time. I didn't want to upset anyone by being interested in who the body was, but I thought it was important the police looked into it. You know, the possibility it could be her."

"I know you didn't, but anything like this tends to get people's backs up. Particularly when there's a history there. People don't always want to be reminded of the past, and it sounds as though this Jessie was a real issue for Cathy."

Helena sighed; she knew David was right even if she didn't want to hear it.

"I think she must have been. I mean, no one has come out and said anything happened between Jessie and Cathy's husband, but it sounds to me as though she was worried something *was* going on. She is too quick to deny it before anyone has even asked her."

David nodded. "It would probably be best just to steer clear for a while. You've only been to a couple of meetings, so it's not like they'll miss you. I'd let it blow over first. Whatever happened back then, she's still upset about it, even though her husband is dead."

Helena sighed and nodded. David was right.

"I was thinking lamb chops for dinner?" he said,

changing the subject as he gathered his paperwork in a messy pile and stuffed it into his work bag.

"Sounds lovely."

David stood up and started to gather the things he needed to make dinner from the fridge. Helena hadn't moved, she just sat there lost in thought. Going through everything that had been said, or indeed not said at the meeting earlier in the day. David turned and looked at her for a moment before speaking.

"I know you feel involved in this, being as you found the body. But I think you should leave this alone for now. Let the police do their work. Then if they do find anything, it won't be you that gets the blame for stirring things up. They are the professionals, after all," David said.

"Yes, you're right, I know you're right. I haven't asked anything else since I saw Sarah the other day. She said pretty much the same thing—leave it to them, they're the ones who will investigate it all. And I will, but I still want to know what happened."

"Of course you do. It's only human nature. What did that Bill chap have to say about it all?" David stopped preparing dinner and stood, drying his hands on a tea towel as they talked.

"Now who's interested?" Helena laughed. She stood up and started to unload the dishwasher as David returned to cooking their meal. "He didn't say a lot, to be honest. I know he knew them all, but I think it was around the time his wife passed away, when there was all the trouble with Jessie and Frank, so he's a bit vague about it all."

They both worked for a few more minutes, in a companionable silence that comes from a long life together, occasionally asking the other to pass something or move something. For the most part, though, they were so used to one another that they communicated the whole time without needing to say a word. Delicious scents started to fill the kitchen as David grilled the chops and put together a salad and some bread rolls. Helena set the table, and once everything was ready, they sat down together to eat.

"When did his wife die?" asked David suddenly.

"Who's?"

"That Bill chap, the one who runs everything."

"You know, I'm not sure, to be honest. He's said a few times it was around the time Jessie left, or went missing, whichever it was. But I'm not sure if it was before or after she went. Why? Do you think it matters?"

"Probably not. Just if she died after Jessie left, then he might know more than if it was before and he was dealing with his grief. I shouldn't imagine he would have had time or energy for anything else when his wife passed away."

She paused eating for a moment, considering what David had said. She couldn't remember Bill mentioning exactly when his wife had passed away, only that it was around then. The chances are he wouldn't remember exactly when Jessie had gone in any case, he must have had more important things to deal with at the time, more important to him at least.

"The problem is there isn't an exact time Jessie left, I don't think, or not one that people seem to be able to remember. Her boyfriend at the time said she didn't turn up to meet him when they were supposed to leave, and I think that was around the last time anyone saw her. But she may have seen her brother after that. I don't think John would have told Murray where Jessie was if she had asked him not to. There was no love lost there. I could phone Murray and ask when it was he last saw her, but I think it might be a bit much. This is delicious, by the way."

"Thanks. Not a bad cook, am I?" he said with a cheeky wink. "No, you'd better not do that, especially as you're not poking around in it anymore, remember?" He gave her a mock stern look and she couldn't help but laugh at the expression on his face.

"Modest too. And no, I'm not going to be causing any more trouble, I promise."

"With that at least," he said with a wink, "you've been trouble one way or another since I first met you."

"Is that why I couldn't get rid of you?"

"I was a poor, innocent young lad when we met. I didn't know what had hit me when you turned up." He grinned.

"I don't remember you complaining." She smiled, even after years together, he could still make her laugh.

"Ah, now, I don't think I've ever said anything about complaining. You were just what a poor innocent young lad needed. It's why I've had a smile on my face ever since." He wiggled his eyebrows at her.

"You talk a lot of rubbish sometimes," she said with a grin.

They finished their meal, with all thoughts of the strange body and Jessie Andrews forgotten about. For that evening at least.

Chapter 15

Helena heard nothing more about the body or Jessie for at least a week. She started to doubt her initial thoughts that Jessie may have passed away, thinking that she could have simply left the area. Slowly, she came to terms with the possibility that she might never uncover the truth about Jessie's disappearance.

She started to question if her mind had fabricated events that didn't actually happen. But one Wednesday morning, two weeks after the fair, everything came flooding back into her mind with a jolt.

Helena had been for her weekly walk around Back Beach. It was the first time she had ventured there since the discovery. Despite the unpleasant memories of her discovery, the scenery was still breathtaking and the solitude comforting. Even so, things had subtly changed now. Although it was still peaceful and relaxing, Helena didn't feel as though she was entirely alone there anymore Almost as though Jessie or whoever the unfortunate person who died there, was with her. There in the air, whispering secrets about what had happened, but just too quietly to be able to hear exactly what was being said—a faint murmur on the breeze. Shaking slightly, she tried not to be so fanciful. A coffee and a sit down before heading back home were just what was needed.

Before making her way back to the main street, she

stood and looked up at the section of the bank where she had first seen the bones. There was no sign of anything there now. The forensic teams had carefully combed the area, no doubt, and removed anything of interest. Even so, Helena couldn't help looking to find a clue as to what had happened there.

It was hard to get a feel for things now. The ground had been so thoroughly raked over and moved about. Even so, Helena was sure the only place the bones could have come from was one of the gardens of the houses on the road above. There were at least two houses that looked over this part of Back Beach and both of their gardens had crumbled away slightly when the bank had slipped. Perhaps Jessie had been killed up there and buried. It made more sense than someone trying to bury a body midway up the incline. When she got the chance, she would try and find out who the houses belonged to, although she was sure they would have changed hands at least once since then.

Sometime around mid-morning, she sat in the cafe with a flat white and a slice of carrot cake. The perfect prescription for a troubled mind. A man she hadn't seen before came into the small cafe. Although Helena wouldn't claim to know everyone who lived locally, many of the people around and about Port Chalmers were people she had seen before and recognized to look at, if not by name or place. The fact she didn't recognize him wasn't the only thing that drew Helena's attention. He looked as though he was in his mid-fifties and although dressed smartly, he would probably be more at home in work clothes. There was something about him that gave him the air of someone who was not entirely comfortable with what he wore now.

He didn't hold her attention for long, and her mind wandered back to Back Beach. However, she was taken by surprise when the man walked over to her table after he had finished talking to the woman at the counter.

"Would you be Helena Statham?" he asked, standing by her table.

Helena was taken aback, not only did he seem to be looking for her, but he knew her name. There was something almost familiar about his voice, but it wasn't something she could immediately place.

"Um, yes. Can I help you?"

"I'm Murray MacPherson. They told me I might find you here. Mind if I sit down?"

Suddenly it became clear to Helena why he might be looking for her, although not what he was doing here in Port Chalmers. She gulped, her throat suddenly feeling dry. She was grateful to be surrounded by people in a busy cafe, rather than being alone somewhere with Murray.

"Not at all," she said, forcing out a smile, and reaching over to move her bag off the other chair at the table so he could join her. She might as well find out what he wanted.

She observed him intently as he took a seat. He didn't match the image she had conjured up in her mind. Possibly because in her mind, Jessie would still be the same age she had been when she had left, and she'd pictured her boyfriend of the time to still be in his early twenties too. It was the age everyone, even her brother remembered her. This man was much older though, a few years older than Helena herself, she thought. He had short hair that looked as though it had once been dark but was now mostly gray. He must have worked outside a good deal, as even now in winter he had a slight tan, and his face had that weathered appearance that comes with long term sun exposure.

"It's nice to meet you, Murray. How can I help you?" She was a little nervous about what he might have to say. Somehow, she didn't think he had come to see her for a friendly chat about the weather or the way the All Blacks had been performing recently.

"I've had to come and give a statement at the police station," he said, "Well, actually, I could have done it in Dunedin or even my local station back home. But I wanted to come back and see Port again, for some reason. All of this has reignited some old memories. Somehow it seemed right to come back to the old place and talk about Jessie here, where I knew her."

Helena nodded encouragingly as he paused. He turned to look around the cafe and out onto the street beyond.

"It looks a bit different since I was last here. Well, I suppose it would after thirty years or so. There are new shops, and this cafe wasn't here then. But it hasn't changed beneath the surface. The people, I mean, they're just the same."

"You haven't been back since?" Helena fiddled with the teaspoon on her saucer, wondering what Murray wanted from her.

"No, I thought about it once or twice, but it seemed best to make a clean break. I didn't want to see Jessie again, not once I'd left. I met my wife a few months later and I didn't want to go backward. I'd moved on."

For a moment they sat in silence. Murray looked lost in thoughts of the past, his youth back in Port Chalmers, and what had happened that made him decide to leave. Helena sat and waited.

"Jessie was eager to get as far away from here as soon as she could. I wanted to go back and take on my uncle's place for him, but it wasn't far enough for her. I think I told you all this on the phone. I was young and in love." He gave a little chuckle and shook his head. "I'd have agreed to most things, completely crazy about her, first real girlfriend and all that. She had this way with her, able to get men young and old dancing to her tune. It was just the women that hated her. I think she just wanted to be loved, to be liked."

"I'm sorry all of this has come up again if it's painful for you," Helena said. Wondering if he had wanted to talk to her and admonish her for bringing up dark memories from his past.

"No, it's not painful. I don't think me and Jessie would have worked out anyway in the end. She was looking for something and I think I fit the bill for a time, but long term I wouldn't have been enough. She would have found someone else once we got out there. No, it had to happen sooner or later. Probably best it was before I'd left and burnt bridges here."

A member of staff from the cafe came over with Murray's coffee and he and Helena paused while she delivered it. Helena waited for him to sort out his drink and then get back to what he wanted to tell her. Once they were left alone again, he started to talk once more.

"I just wanted to see who it was who decided to look into what happened to her. I thought about it, and it seemed strange no one had questioned where she'd gone before. John was pretty cut up when she just left. I think I told you I went round there to see what had happened to her, if she was still at home?"

Helena nodded encouragingly.

"Well, when he found out her things were gone, he rushed at me, pinned me up against one of those barns, demanding to know where she was. It seems strange now after that he just accepted she'd left. Then there's Bill. His wife had been sick for ages, and he'd been sniffing around Jessie for Mrs. Harding mark two, if you ask me. She was young enough to be his daughter, well, it seemed like that at the time. Certainly too young for him."

"Was she interested in him like that?" Helena asked, surprised at this information.

Murray paused to consider it for a second, as though it was something he hadn't thought about before.

"At the time I would have said not a chance. We used to laugh about him and that Frank chap behind their backs. I don't know though, I don't think she was interested in him, or anything happened, but she was very good at telling people what they wanted to hear. But the same goes for me as well as for them, doesn't it? They both may well have believed she was interested, just like I thought she'd go away with me. Who knows what she said to them about our relationship. Either way, I don't know if Frank would have left his wife though. Is he still with the old battle-axe?"

Murray hadn't kept up to date with what had been happening with the people in his old hometown it seemed.

"Cathy? Well, she died a few years ago now, but I think they stayed together until the end."

He nodded. "Cathy, that's it. She hated Jessie with

a passion. I think Jessie might have even tried it on with Frank just to get her back up. I don't know if there was anything but a bit of flirting, to be honest, and she flirted with everyone. Bill was different though. His wife died the day before Jessie vanished and I think Jessie worried once she was gone, he might try and force the issue with her. That's one of the reasons she was so keen to leave then. We hadn't finalized a date. In those last couple of weeks, she seemed suddenly keen to organize it all and get out of here. I don't know what changed to make her so anxious to suddenly get away, but I couldn't help feeling she was running away from something or someone, maybe."

Jessie didn't sound like the nicest girl, leading all of these men on. Helena paused for a moment, not sure how to put her thoughts into words that wouldn't upset Murray. He'd cared for the young woman at one time.

"She sounds as though she might have been a bit of trouble," she suggested tentatively.

"No, not really. We did laugh at them all behind their backs, but they were old enough to know better, trying it on with a girl who was little more than a kid. Her dad was so strict with her. I know he used to hit John and her mum. I think Jessie got the worst of it too from time to time." He shook his head with a grim frown. "It's not an excuse, but she seemed to always get the rough end of things. As soon as she realized, she was getting attention, any kind of attention, she reveled in it. The women hated the way she looked, and those old men only wanted her for one thing. I think she just decided to make the most of it when she could."

Helena picked up her coffee and drank the rest of it, considering what he'd said for a second. She wasn't entirely sure why Murray was telling her all of this. It's not as though she was involved in the investigation herself, no more than as an old busybody nosing into everyone's business.

"Was there a reason you wanted to see me and tell me all of this? Or just because I asked questions the other day?" Helena asked, almost worried to hear what he'd say.

"There were two reasons. I wanted to see who had finally looked into what had happened to her, when none of us, the people who supposedly cared about her back then, ever considered it."

"And the other reason?" Helena prompted.

This time he paused as though not sure if he wanted to mention this second reason. "I understand you're friendly with John?"

"Jessie's brother? I don't know if I'd say friendly as such. I've been up to his place a couple of times, but I don't really know him. I only met him for the first time a few weeks ago, why?"

She frowned. What had her knowing John got to do with Murray wanting to speak to her?

"The policewoman I spoke to mentioned it was you who'd been to see him first and found out about Jessie. I thought you might be able to speak to him for me?" he asked.

"I can try? You can't speak to him yourself?"

"No. John never did like me. Even before all of this, we were the same year at school and there was no love lost between us. He hated me after she was gone. It's not important, but I'd still like to know something. When Jessie left, did she take her diary with her?"

"Diary? She kept one?" This was the first Helena

had heard of a diary. John hadn't mentioned it, which didn't necessarily mean much, but if he still had the diary, he would possibly have said something about it when they were talking about the postcards. Something like that could help find out what had happened.

"Yes, she was fanatical about that. I don't want to see it or anything. It's just for my peace of mind. You see, if she was planning on leaving, then she would have packed it, there's no way she would have left it in that house. I never read it, but I know there were all sorts in there, about her relationship with her father, what she thought about everyone, and things like that. But if she left it, then she didn't plan to leave. Someone took her clothes maybe, but without the diary, she didn't pack them herself."

"So you think if the diary was left behind then it shows she didn't leave, and the body could be her?" Helena asked, considering this. Someone else could have taken the diary to make it seem as though she was gone, but they would have had to know about the diary. How common knowledge had this diary been?

Murray considered this for a second. If it was still around then it might have plenty of clues to share about what had happened to Jessie. But then the police would surely have it by now. Of course, John might deny all knowledge of the book, not wanting people to know his sister's secrets.

"I don't know. She could have packed planning to go with me and then something happened. If it's still there, then I think she didn't intend to go anywhere. I suppose what I want to know is, for my ego at least, was she serious about going away with me, even if she didn't meet me."

Murray claimed he was not bothered anymore by what had happened. That the past being brought up again hadn't affected him, but clearly, it wasn't completely true. Helena wondered if he was more upset than he was letting on, or if this was just him wanting to know what had happened to his girlfriend all of those years ago. Tying up the loose ends from his past and putting to bed questions that had been left unanswered after she vanished.

"I'll see if I can ask him. I've still got your number if he tells me anything, so I can let you know. I don't know him well though, so don't expect miracles. He might not want to tell me or might not even know what I'm talking about, but I will ask him when I next see him. I'll see if I can get out there again soon."

"Thank you. And, if you do find out what happened to her, you will let me know?"

"Of course. I think the police are more likely to get somewhere with that kind of thing than me though."

Murray picked up his cup and swallowed the remains of his coffee before standing up, ready to leave.

"You said you'd had a row when I spoke to you before and that's why you weren't surprised when she didn't turn up?" she asked before he headed out of the building.

A dark look passed over his face for a moment before he answered. "A row? No, I don't think so."

"Oh, I thought that was why you weren't surprised she didn't turn up to meet you?"

"Maybe, I don't know. We were always having little arguments about something; it didn't mean anything with Jessie. We'd fall out one minute and then the next it would all be fine again—it was just the way she was."

Helena nodded. She knew people like that. Somehow, though, she couldn't help but feel it wasn't the whole story here. Murry seemed to be in a hurry to leave now, as though he didn't want her to keep asking questions.

"I'll let you know if I find out anything about the diary then," Helena said.

"Thank you," he said. "See you."

With that, he headed for the door and out onto the street. Helena sat for a few moments, thinking about how much trouble a girl who hadn't been seen for thirty years seemed to have stirred up. Not that Helena was entirely innocent when it came to stirring up old memories.

Chapter 16

Their conversation left Helena feeling a little uneasy and wanting to return home, to think about everything he had told her. As she started walking up the road toward where the car was parked, she noticed a group of people gathered on the other side of the street. She didn't give it much attention, her mind absorbed with Jessie, Murray, and all that had gone on thirty years ago. But drawing closer, she heard two men arguing while a couple of other people stood to one side watching them. Helena had no desire to join the onlookers, treating the disagreement like an entertaining street show or TV drama. She hustled back to her car, disregarding the chaos, until a sudden increase in volume caught her attention and caused her to stop.

"What makes you think I have any idea what happened to Jessie anyway?" came a shout from one of the two men.

Helena looked over and realized one of the men was Murray. The other man's back was to her, but there was something familiar about him too. She turned to get a better look. The second man turned his head slightly and immediately noticed it was John. She'd been told by a few people that John hardly ever came into Port Chalmers these days, and she couldn't remember having run into him before. To see him not only here, but arguing with Murray in the middle of the street came as a bit of surprise.

Curious as to what was being said, Helena wandered over to the other side of the road and walked a little bit closer. She felt somewhat responsible for bringing all of these painful feelings back to the front of everyone's minds and for bringing Murray back to the town. The two men were too busy shouting at one another to pay her any attention.

"I came to see you after she didn't turn up. She was supposed to meet me and leave with me, but she didn't. Do you think I ran off with her and then came back to ask you where she was?" Murray shouted, his arms gesturing in the air. Anger was clear in his words, sounding perhaps more frustrated than anything violent. Whatever the emotion behind the argument, it was clear there was a danger of it spilling over into something far more serious.

"I don't know what you did. She was there in the morning. That was the last time I saw her. She told me she was going to see you and then I never saw her again. You must have known what happened to her. I always knew you were no good for her," said John, his voice shaking slightly with the force of emotion, and although angry, he sounded like he was on the verge of breaking down. Finally, the uncertainty and questions over what had happened to his sister all those years ago had risen to the surface when he ran into Murray again.

Helena was concerned about his appearance. He seemed more wild-looking than Murray. His short hair was rumpled, and his clothes had a disheveled look as though he'd slept in them the previous night, if indeed, he'd had any sleep at all. Had he been drinking, or was the agitation purely down to his emotional state?

"You were just jealous. Just because I got her out of the farm and thinking of a life away from here. You couldn't stand it. You or your father. You just wanted to keep her at home, wrapped in cotton wool away from the world. You all knew what she was like, but there was nothing you could do about it."

"She wasn't like that until she met you. You corrupted her. She was sweet and innocent until you came along." John pointed his finger aggressively at Murray's chest, as though to highlight each word he spoke.

"Ha, we both know that's a lie. Jessie loved the male attention she got long before I was with her. She'd even got half of your father's friends following her around with their tongues hanging out when she was little more than a kid."

John looked outraged. "My sister was an innocent young girl, I looked after her."

Although they were still arguing, they weren't shouting as much as they had been, and the other observers started to drift away, perhaps self-conscious about being seen paying too much attention to what was clearly a private dispute between the two men. Helena found herself alone, watching them, wondering if she should say something. It didn't look as though they were going to physically attack one another, and perhaps this was something they both needed to get off their chest. Still, she couldn't help feeling this was all her fault and she should be stepping in and taking them to somewhere a bit more private than the middle of the main street to have this out.

"Innocent? I was a choir boy compared to your

sister. I loved her, as much as you love anyone when you're that age, but she was no innocent, and it wasn't me who had corrupted her," said Murray.

John appeared to age rapidly before Helena's eyes, his once defiant stance now slumped as if all strength had drained from his body. When it became obvious there was nothing left to be said, Murray shook his head and walked briskly away from John, leaving him standing alone on the pavement. John stared after him as he walked away, Helena wasn't sure he was watching him though, he seemed to be somewhere else, in a different time.

"John?" she asked softly, walking a little closer and putting her hand on his arm.

He turned to her, a confused look on his face, as though he wasn't sure how he'd ended up there on the footpath by the war memorial in the center of Port Chalmers. His face looked blank and lost. Now closer to him, she couldn't smell any alcohol on his breath.

"Are you all right?" she asked. "Do you want to get a coffee or go and sit down for a minute?"

"I, um, no, I'm fine." He looked at her as though just registering her presence. "Helena? What are you doing here?"

"I was just in town and saw you. I thought I'd come over and see if you were all right." She decided it best not to mention the argument she'd witnessed with Murray only moments before. John appeared disorientated and reasoned that bringing up the argument would only make matters worse.

"I'm fine. I just, it's just all of this talk of Jessie, it's stirred all of these memories up and then *he* is here. I thought he'd left long ago." John gestured in the direction Murray had gone. "You heard him?"

"I heard something, but not all the details. I didn't want to intrude."

She led John over to the seats in the small garden area where the war memorial stood. It was a cold day but getting him to sit down for a few minutes seemed like the best idea. He still didn't seem to wholly be himself, and no doubt needed a few minutes to pull himself together and recover from the encounter.

"He ruined her life, you know? If he hadn't come along then she wouldn't have got all of these ideas about leaving us. She would still be here now, and nothing would have changed. He might not have been involved directly in whatever happened to her, but it was still all his fault. I blame him for everything. I always did."

"What makes you say that?" she asked. It certainly wasn't the impression she'd been given by other people who had talked about Jessie. Nobody else seemed to have thought anyone had corrupted Jessie or influenced her. As far as she had been able to tell, it had been Jessie who had been influencing and encouraging other people. But then her older brother was bound to have seen Jessie in a more favorable light.

"She'd had boyfriends before him. She was a good-looking, popular girl. But he was a bit older, and I think she thought he was exciting or thrilling or something. She started to stay out later, even nights when she didn't come back home at all. I covered for her. Our father was very strict after Mum died; he kept us close to home. We'd cover for one another, though. I was older so able to go out more, but I'd often end up staying in and telling Dad that Jessie was still at home too. He worked late on the farm and when she was at home, she tended to stay in her room out of the way."

He stopped for a minute, lost in memories of his youth. Helena waited patiently for him to continue. So far, it sounded much like any other teenager's story. They reached an age where they thought they knew best and wanted to do as they pleased, to try and break away from parental control. Especially when, as appeared to have been the case for Jessie, the parent was very strict and overbearing.

"We used to take it in turns, but once Murray came along, she was out every night. I think Dad had an idea she was going off the rails. He tried to encourage her to get involved in the local church youth group. She hated it to begin with, but once she met the men who ran it, she changed. Suddenly, she seemed eager to go. Flirting with them one night and then out with Murray the next. Dad thought she was just going to church meetings and staying in, but she was getting wilder and wilder all the time."

"The men at the church?"

"Bill and Frank. Bill was involved in everything back then, and Frank used to follow in his footsteps. They should have known better, a young girl like that, young enough to be their daughter. She was only a few years older than Frank's son."

There they were again, the older men who appeared to have some connection with Jessie. Every time someone spoke about Jessie back then, both Frank and Bill were mentioned too. It seemed everyone knew something was going on there. It was no wonder Cathy was so against Jessie, even now. As she thought about everything, learned something suddenly occurred to

Helena.

"Your father was still alive when Jessie went missing. I'm surprised he didn't try and find her, being as he was quite protective?"

"I wondered myself for a while. He got sick pretty soon after she left, which didn't help, but I think he was glad in some ways she had gone away. Left behind everything that was happening. I think he thought she'd go away for a few months or a year or so and be back. The first postcard came soon after she left and, although he was mad, he accepted she'd gone off and done her own thing. I don't know, maybe the strain of looking after a headstrong teenage daughter with no wife to help had just got too much for him and he was glad of the break. He died just over a year after she left. He might have tried to track her down when she didn't come home."

Helena nodded, not entirely convinced by this explanation, but not having an alternative one she wanted to suggest. John seemed a little more composed and more like the man she met at his house. Still, she was a little nervous about bringing up the question Murray had wanted her to ask.

"I spoke to Murray earlier," she began.

John lifted his head and looked at her.

"He mentioned some diary of Jessie's. He said she wouldn't have gone anywhere without it. I just wondered if she'd left it behind?"

"No, not that I ever found. I suppose Dad could have found it and destroyed it, but I don't think he even knew she had it. He wouldn't have known where she kept it. I did look, a few months after she'd gone when she still hadn't come back, but I didn't see it anywhere.

I'd thought maybe there might be some clues as to where she had gone written in it. I missed her too. I wanted some kind of connection with her, but it wasn't there. I just assumed she'd taken it with her. He's right, she wouldn't have willingly left it." He shook his head as he spoke.

Helena thought about this for a minute. Would Jessie have left her diary behind if she was as attached to it as her brother and boyfriend at the time seemed to be claiming? Helena hadn't kept a diary herself as a teenager, but she knew people who had. They were usually well protected and never shared with prying eyes, but then both men seemed to have known about its existence, which was itself unusual.

"Did you ever read her diary?" Helena asked.

"No, she kept it to herself. She sometimes used to read out passages to me, her thoughts about people we both knew or had met, but she did it less as she got older. She had a sharp wit and could see things about people that weren't always obvious."

"How do you mean?"

"I don't know if she could see people more clearly or what it was, but she was quite funny. She could describe someone to a T, picking up on the little things that made them who they were. Often, it was things you hadn't even noticed, but when she mentioned them, they were always spot on and suddenly so obvious you knew exactly what she meant." He broke into a smile as he remembered some things his sister must have shared with him. Helena could see they had been very close, once upon a time.

Helena could see how Jessie could have upset some people with her possibly less-than-flattering descriptions. Add that to the girl who liked to keep men following her every whim, then already there was a picture of someone who might not be very well-liked. The way people had reacted to her memory was becoming less and less surprising.

"Did people get upset about the things she said?" Helena asked.

"They usually didn't know. She could be biting and sharp with her descriptions and more often than not, they weren't very kind. She was always popular though. People wouldn't have liked what she had thought about them if they'd known, but it was a different face she presented to them."

Helena nodded. The more she learned about Jessie, the less clear things became. There were many reasons why she might have wanted to leave the area. Perhaps she'd upset one too many people and made a clean start elsewhere. Of course, it was just as easy to consider that she may well have upset the wrong person and they had taken matters into their own hands to deal with her.

"She was far from perfect, but she was my sister and I loved her," John said. He gave Helena a sad smile and stood up. "Thank you for listening to my ramblings. I need to get back to the farm. I'm not even sure what I came here for now."

With that, Helena bid him goodbye and he headed slowly off back toward the side of the road, to where Helena could see his car parked. She had learned plenty today, but she wasn't sure that any of it helped her to get any answers.

Chapter 17

When she got back home, Helena searched the local council rates database to see who owned the two houses that overlooked Back Beach. It wasn't a very fruitful search. One had been sold twice in the last five years and before that, there was no record of who had owned it. The other was a rental property, owned by some investment firm based in Auckland. They had only had it for ten years or so and there were no details of any previous owners. There was a good chance it had been a rental property in the past too. Any number of people could have lived there since Jessie went missing. It was something she would just have to leave to the police. It seemed silly now, thinking that she might have discovered something that the police had missed. She closed the lid of her laptop and slid it under the sofa, giving up on that line of inquiry.

"How was your walk?" David asked as he came to sit next to Helena on the sofa. "Did you make it to Back Beach or decide to go somewhere else after what happened last time?"

He shook his head and raised an eyebrow as he leaned forward to pick up the television remote, repeating his question.

"Sorry, what was that? I was miles away," Helena said, suddenly registering he was there and had been talking to her.

"Obviously. I was just asking about your walk today if you'd been around Back Beach or not, this afternoon?"

"Yes, it was quite nice, actually, no sign of what happened before. I was a bit worried it was going to ruin it for me, but it didn't."

"So, you weren't just thinking about the body you found again then?" David asked, a slight grin playing around his mouth.

"Am I that obvious?" she said, laughing.

"Well, it's all you've been thinking about since you found her, let's be honest."

"True. I ran into John and Murray today in Port." She turned toward him and tucked her leg up under her, getting comfortable, eager to discuss all she had learned recently.

"Murray? Who's Murray?"

"Remember, he was Jessie's boyfriend? He used to work at the garage. He doesn't live here anymore, but came to see the police about something, now they're seriously looking at the idea the body might be Jessie."

While Helena had been living and breathing the mystery since she'd found the body, David hadn't committed all of the details to memory quite the way she had. She tried to hide her irritation that he wasn't immediately recalling the things she'd shared with him so far.

"And he came to see you? Are you sure you're not getting too involved in all of this? It worries me you stirring all of this up?"

Helena should have known he would have said that.

"No, he didn't come to see me exactly. He ran into

me in the cafe, but I suppose he was sort of looking for me."

Helena frowned, remembering their conversation. Was it normal for someone to be so interested in a girlfriend they had broken up with thirty years ago? If she was honest, she could barely remember the men she had been seeing at that age. It was a lifetime ago. But then, none of her boyfriends had vanished off the face of the earth the way Jessie seemed to have done. Then there was the question of the argument he had mentioned. When she'd brought it up again today, Murray had brushed it off as being nothing important. Was he just trying to put her off?

"I've been having a few thoughts about who could be responsible for what happened." She held up her hand, sensing Dave's objection. "I know you don't want me to get more involved, but I've met all of these people and I can't help wondering about them."

Dave frowned. "Have they confirmed the body is Jessie?"

"No. I think they are waiting for DNA confirmation or something, but I think it's looking pretty likely. It would all make sense anyway; I can't imagine who else it could be."

Dave nodded. Things often seemed to become public knowledge long before there was any kind of official announcement.

"I'm not going to do anything, but let me tell you what I've been thinking," she said.

"All right, but let me get us a drink first, give me a minute." He stood up. "Coffee? Or would you prefer wine?"

"There's a bottle of red open still, isn't there? We

may as well finish that."

While he was getting the drinks, she considered all of the people she had met over the last couple of weeks. She couldn't help but think even though Jessie had died so long ago, the people who were involved were still around now. It seemed strange somehow to think one of the people she'd been spending time with recently might be a killer. She could understand Dave's concern, but it didn't seem real. She might be able to think about who might have been involved, but the idea one of them was a killer and might be a danger to her, that was something she just couldn't quite get her head around.

"Here," Dave said, handing a glass and settling back down on the sofa with his own drink.

"Cheers." Helena took a sip and then set the glass down, sorting out her thoughts.

"The more I learn about Jessie and what went on before she left, the more I'm sure there's someone that's still here, that I've met, who had something to do with it," she said.

David shook his head. "And that's why I've been worried about you getting too involved in all of this. If people you've been talking to were part of what happened, then it could be dangerous."

"Yes, I know." She sighed impatiently. "It's not that I've not been listening to you, or don't know something could happen, I just can't help trying to get to the bottom of what's been going on."

He reached out and gave her knee a little squeeze. "I know, sweetheart, I just worry about you. I don't know if I would be any different if it had been me who found her. I don't know what I'd do if anything happened to you."

Helena gave him a tight smile; she knew how he felt.

"What would I tell the boys? Sorry, your mother has gone and got herself murdered, sticking her nose into things again," he said with a grin, lightening the mood. "I'm sure they could understand how it might happen."

She laughed and hit him lightly on the arm. "I'm sure even they could see the difference between me trying to find out who murdered someone thirty years ago and me interrogating them about where they were going when they were teenagers!" She laughed at the thought.

"You think someone you've met recently might have killed her, then?" David asked, brows furrowed.

"I don't know. They all seem connected to her and possibly have a reason to kill her. I'm sure it must be her; I don't see who else it could be. I mean, think about it, how likely is it there's another missing girl at around the same time?"

"True." David nodded. "You did tell me she was a difficult girl, though. Is it possible she couldn't have killed someone herself? I don't know, accidentally after some kind of row over a boyfriend or something and then disappeared because of it?"

Helena rubbed her hand across her face wearily. "It's not impossible. I mean, I did think about that, but it just doesn't seem very likely somehow. If someone else was missing as well, then I'm sure it would have come up before now. There were reasons Jessie wasn't reported as missing at the time. I can't believe she would be able to be involved in someone's death, hide the fact this person was also missing, and be able to vanish so easily herself. Surely there's far too much luck involved in that scenario. In any case, who could it be?"

"No, you're right, it doesn't sound very likely. How old was she in any case?"

"Jessie? Nineteen or twenty-something like that, not very old."

"Yeah, you're right, barely more than a kid. Most of them barely know what time of day it is, let alone managing to kill someone, hide the body, disappear, and then make it look like this person wasn't missing. Certainly, none of my students would manage that," David said with a chuckle.

"No, the more I think about it, the more sure I am it must be Jessie and I think the police are thinking the same. I don't think they would be interviewing Murray or John or anyone else that knew her at the time if they weren't fairly sure that's who the body is."

Helena paused to take another sip of wine, letting her mind run for a few moments over the people she'd been talking to who knew Jessie.

"So, do you think her brother was in some way to blame? John, is it?" David asked, breaking the silence.

"I don't know. I did wonder about John. I mean, he never reported her as missing, no one else did either, but he would have found it easy to put everyone off and make them believe she'd gone away. But would he have gone to all the trouble of getting someone to send him the cards?"

"The postcards? How do you know he even got them through the post? Surely, he could have faked them quite easily."

"Maybe. I don't know. I mean he possibly could

have done it, but some of them look old, not done recently. It would have meant he faked them over a long period, and why bother? He could have just said she called him from time to time or something if anyone ever asked." She paused for a minute, thinking it over. "I mean, that would be the obvious thing to do. He didn't even need to mention her to me. I don't think anyone else would have brought her up—most of them seem to be pleased she left."

"Poor girl, it's all a bit sad, isn't it?"

"Yeah, I know she caused a few issues, but I can't help but feel sorry for her." Helena sighed. "I think she was looking for love and acceptance, from the things John's told me. Their father struggled with her and with her mum dead, I think she was just a bit lost. Even John doesn't seem to have been able to help her much and when he talks about her, it's obvious he loved his sister."

David leaned forward and picked up the photograph of Jessie that Helena had left on the coffee table in front of them. He looked at it for a minute before shaking his head and putting it back down.

"So, if not John, then who? That Bill chap?"

"I did wonder about him too. He's been pretty cagey about it, but I think he had feelings for her, a bit of an inappropriate crush. She was a pretty young thing who showed him lots of attention and at a time when he was probably feeling quite alone himself."

"You're not falling for all of that 'my wife doesn't understand me' guff some men trot out, are you?" David asked with an incredulous laugh.

"Ha, no, but his wife was very sick at the time—she died around then. I'm not excusing it, but it might explain why he was a bit more susceptible to her attention."

Helena couldn't remember if anyone had said exactly when it was that Bill's wife had passed away. In all honesty, she couldn't recall much about her at all. She knew she'd been sick and died around then, but she couldn't remember what had been wrong with her, or indeed if anyone had actually said. Had she been like Cathy and Diane? Helping Bill with all of his many community groups and committees? Perhaps his wife had been less willing to get involved, especially if she hadn't been well. Helena wondered how she had felt about Jessie. Was it possible she had been jealous, could she have been responsible for what happened? But if she was unwell, it didn't seem likely. If only she knew what had happened to Bill's wife if she had been well enough to attack the younger woman and bury her body. She might have to ask someone how she had died and exactly when it had happened.

"Who does that leave then?" David asked. "If not Bill or John, who else was there?"

"Well, there's a couple of people who aren't around anymore. Bill's wife, but as I said, she died around then too. Cathy's husband was quite taken with her at the time too. But he's dead as well. Of course, then there's Cathy and Diane themselves. Oh, and Jessie's boyfriend Murray."

"And do you think any of them could be involved? The boyfriend has got to be likely, no?"

"It would make sense, I suppose. You would think he got sick of her flirting with everyone else, not just the older men, and they had an argument which went wrong?"

"Maybe. She does seem to have been leading everyone on a merry dance. What happened after she left, has anyone told you?"

Helen cast her mind back over the conversations she had with Murray and also what John had said about his sister's boyfriend. He hadn't stayed in the area long after Jessie had left. Murray had told her they had already been planning on leaving for Australia and then she hadn't turned up.

"They were supposed to go to Australia together, but she didn't meet him when she was supposed to. I think he might have tried to find out what had happened from John, but they just didn't get on, and John was just pleased Jessie had left without Murray."

"Yes, but who's to say that's true? John thought Jessie had left for Australia, so I assume she had packed ready to go?" David asked.

"Yes." Helena tried to remember exactly what she had been told. "Jessie had packed a load of her things according to John. If he's telling the truth, then she certainly planned to leave, and I assume at that stage, she was planning to meet Murray. I thought something must have happened to her when she was on the way to meet him, but maybe it didn't. Maybe she did meet Murray, after all."

"You think they met, argued, and Murray killed her, by accident or maybe even in a fit of rage? Then all he had to do was get rid of her things and pretend she had never shown up."

Helena considered the idea. She liked Murray and hoped that's not what happened. She didn't like to think she had been so wrong about him.

"But then why would he have gone to John trying

to find Jessie? I mean, it might have thrown people off the scent about them meeting up, but it could have backfired and made people try and find out where she had gone."

"That's true," Dave agreed. "Maybe he wasn't thinking straight and thought it was the best way to throw the scent off him. It did work after all."

"Yes, even so, I think he would have just left himself, that had been the plan if they had met up, so he could have just disappeared at the same time and the chances are no one would have tried to track them down. He could have just said they'd split up later and she'd gone her own way."

"I'm not sure, to be honest," Dave said. "I still think you're expecting someone to act rationally when something pretty major has happened. It's worth thinking that Murray could be involved. I'd feel safer if you stayed away from him anyway."

Helena wasn't convinced. It wasn't just her own feelings about Murray, although that did play a large part in shaping her suspicions. But if it weren't Murray or any of the others, they had discussed, then who was it? Helena couldn't shake the feeling she had met the person who was responsible, or who knew the person involved, at the very least. There was always Cathy and Diane. It was funny, she often thought of them as one person, as though if one of them were guilty, then they both would be, but of course, that wasn't very likely. They were just friends and possibly hadn't even been as close back then when their husbands were both still alive. But they were worth considering more closely.

"Then there's Cathy and Diane," she said, voicing her thoughts.

"Who are they? The women you met at that meeting and fair you went to?" David asked.

"Cathy's the one whose husband was, from what I can gather, a bit of a fan of Jessie's. He's dead now, but I think he used to enjoy her attention. She hasn't got a good thing to say about Jessie, and she was so adamant her husband, Frank, wasn't interested in her. I felt certain that he must have been."

"So, she might be a bit of a strong contender herself, then? This Cathy?"

"Yes, well, she certainly didn't even like Jessie's name being mentioned when I brought it up."

But it raised another question—if Cathy had been involved in Jessie's death, would she still be so angry toward her? She wasn't sure. Cathy's anger was certainly strong enough to have survived for thirty years, but would that have been the case if she had been responsible for Jessie's death?

"There is another possibility there," Helena said, thinking aloud. "If Cathy's husband were responsible in some way for what happened, it might explain why Cathy is still so angry now, blaming Jessie for what happened."

"How do you mean?" David asked, confused.

"If he'd got upset over something, felt she'd been leading him on or something like that, let his jealousy get the better of him, then he might have been the one who killed Jessie. He's dead now, I don't know how or when he passed away, but perhaps it was something to do with his guilt over what happened, and then Cathy hasn't been able to get over it. I don't know. Does that sound too far-fetched?"

David was quiet as he considered for a moment.

"Perhaps. I don't think it's an impossible idea, but you're just working on guesswork there. I don't know why Cathy would still be so angry about Jessie, but it is one possibility. It might be difficult to find out anything about her husband seeing as he's dead now, and I'm not sure asking her too many questions would be a good idea. What about the other one you mentioned?"

"Diane? To be honest I know even less about her."

Although Diane had been at the meeting and the fair, she hadn't stood out in Helena's mind in any way. She sat quietly, backing up whatever Cathy said. It was clear the two women had known each other for a long time. But that didn't mean anything. She didn't know Diane had any reason to wish Jessie ill. But she must have been around at the time all of this was happening. What had happened to her husband? She'd the impression Diane had been married and he was no longer around, but couldn't remember anyone actually telling her that. It was just the feeling she got. Perhaps he had been as keen on Jessie as Cathy's husband. If the story had been similar there, it might have been Diane who acted in anger and that was why she seemed less bothered now.

"There's a chance she's in some way involved, I don't know how. I don't even know what happened to her husband, but I might try to find out." She caught David's expression. "Subtly. I won't put myself in any danger. I don't think she could be involved anyway, to be honest."

"It doesn't sound to me as though you're any further forward. It could be any of these people you've mentioned. I don't want to go on, but I think you are probably better off leaving it with the police."

"You're probably right. I don't like the idea someone I've met and chatted to could have killed someone. Just seems too far-fetched."

"It might be best if you just keep away from all of them for a while until the police have had time to investigate things properly and get to the bottom of it all," David said, standing up and picking up their empty wine glasses.

"Yes, I will, after tomorrow's meeting." She glanced at him sheepishly.

"What meeting?" he said with a long-suffering sigh.

"It's just a final meeting about the fair that I did. I won't be on my own with anyone and it's at the hall in Port Chalmers, so I can't see there being a problem. I'm going to have to at least show my face, seeing as I helped out at the fair. That will be it then, I promise."

David shook his head with a wry smile, and Helena couldn't help but grin back at him. She knew he was only concerned for her safety, but she didn't think he needed to worry. She'd been letting her imagination run away with her, acting like she was one of those detectives on TV she enjoyed watching so much. She'd go to the meeting tomorrow and then take a bit of a break from all of this being part of the community stuff. It had been more eventful than she imagined.

"Bedtime?" Dave asked, coming back into the room.

"Yeah, I think so. I could do with a good night's sleep."

Chapter 18

After the rather disastrous meeting the previous week, Helena didn't really want to go back and join in with the fair committee. It had been bad enough feeling like she had been the cause of Cathy and then Diane walking out of the meeting, but Bill had also clearly been upset by everything. After seeing Murray and John arguing in the street, she began to think she was causing more and more problems all over the place. It seemed wherever she went and whatever she did caused upset and discord. Perhaps it would be better to avoid everyone for a while until everything had settled down a bit.

Bill's message had flashed across her phone the day before, urging her to meet him in the hall once again to discuss the funds they had raised. Initially, Helena had decided not to go. The thought of sitting there being the object of Cathy's hatred or being ignored by the group didn't fill her with much joy. But her motive for getting involved wasn't just to unravel the unfolding mystery, but to get a bit more involved locally. It was with this in mind, a week after the aborted post fair meeting, she found herself sitting at the small table in the hall once more.

On the whole, she had spent much of her adult life avoiding committees and the like. She had heard too many horror stories of the way these local groups could descend into anarchy. Usually, sane members could find themselves consumed with an attack of megalomania as they attempted to grab all of the power and influence (such as it was) for themselves. People who had been involved with organizations tended to be wary of new members with fresh ideas. She'd seen it happen before with groups set up at work. Local committee politics was something she was just going to have to deal with if she wanted to help out, and the fair members seemed at least to be relatively safe so far. Unless one of them was the murderer, of course.

"I think we can give ourselves a pat on the back. Well done everyone. We raised fourteen hundred dollars, which is nothing to be sneezed at and is significantly up on last year's figure," said Bill, reading from the bank statement in front of him. The other members of the committee nodded in approval but didn't say anything.

Bill sat once more at the head of the table, with Cathy and Diane on either side of him. Helena had chosen a seat next to Diane further down the table. She had worried about how Cathy might have reacted to her this week, but it was almost as though her previous outburst had never even happened. Cathy was polite and civil, and Helena was left trying to decide if this was because all had been forgiven, or because Cathy had decided to try to kill her with kindness. She didn't feel she knew the woman well enough as yet to make an accurate assessment as to which way it might go. Keeping quiet and nodding and smiling at the right interval would probably be the safest choice for now.

Diane tended to take a back seat at the previous meetings Helena had been to. She didn't seem to say much herself, letting either Cathy or Bill take the lead. Helena would be interested to see if there was more to her when the others weren't there. She tried to talk to her on a couple of occasions, but Diane didn't seem to want to stick around for long. Or at least not without Cathy being there with her. It wouldn't have even surprised Helena if Diane didn't really mind one way or another about the meetings, but Cathy had pushed her into being there.

"I've banked all of the money now and a cheque will be sent to cancer research this weekend. I'll get you to write out the cheque please, Diane. Would anyone like to second that?" Bill asked. Diane raised her hand whilst Cathy made notes, taking down the meeting minutes.

"Yes, of course, I've got the checkbook," Diane said, routing around in her rather voluminous leather bag. She pulled out knitting, paperwork, a bag of peppermints and other odds and ends looking for but failing to find the elusive checkbook.

Again, Helena was struck by how this was Bill's show. It seemed Diane and Cathy filled the roles of secretary and treasurer, at least in name, but Bill took on everything else. While it may only be a small group who met to fundraise for various causes and charities, she couldn't help but feel it filled some larger role for him. As a retired man with no wife or children in his life, she wondered what else he had, other than these groups and committees he was so busy with.

"I don't think there's much else we need to cover in this meeting," he said, looking around at the three women. "I know we're looking to do a cake sale later in the year for the local school and there was talk of a raffle for the wildlife hospital, but I think we can wait for the next meeting to start discussing those."

Helena nodded along with the others and wondered again if her presence was necessary.

Cathy and Diane gathered their things and headed to the door. After wishing them both goodbye, Helena remained at the table with Bill. She had hung around for a few minutes wanting to catch him alone and make sure all was well between them. Although they had all been acting as though everything had been forgotten., Bill had been so welcoming when she'd first offered to join the group.

"I'm glad you've decided to keep coming along and helping our little group," Bill said with a smile.

"Yes, I enjoyed the fair and I still have plenty of time on my hands, so I thought I'd keep coming. Is it only usually the three of you at the meetings?"

"Ah, yes. It is these days. There used to be a bigger group, but you know how it is—people don't have the time for this kind of thing anymore. Some just aren't the right kind of people too."

Helena raised her eyebrows. Surely any help would be welcome, or was this the local politics in committees she'd heard so much about coming into play? She couldn't help but wonder if this wasn't some kind of sly dig at her, being as she'd been the cause of the problems previously.

"Oh yes, all kinds of ideas about what we should or shouldn't be doing. You wouldn't believe the people who come along after just one meeting and want to change everything we've ever done as though they have all of the answers and know everything already."

Helena shifted nervously, trying to remember if

she'd suggested any new ideas on a couple of occasions she'd attended.

"I can imagine," she said, trying to sound sympathetic, while not having a clue what he was talking about.

"Of course, we'd love to have more people helping us. It's always the same ones who get involved in this kind of thing, but I always say, if you can't rely on yourself, then you can't rely on anyone." He chuckled.

Helena considered this for a minute. Bill had the air of a martyr, but she couldn't help feeling he loved every second of being part of the group. It was often the way though, to complain about others' lack of involvement, but be unwilling to hand over control of anything to anyone else. Loving every second of being the one in charge of everything—she'd come across that type at work before.

"I was a bit worried about coming along this week," Helena said, deciding to fish for a bit of information about how Cathy and Diane felt about her. He nodded as she spoke.

"After last week? I wouldn't worry about it. We were all a bit upset about everything being brought up again, but it wasn't your fault. It all seems to be forgotten again now."

Helena nodded and smiled. She hadn't realized she had been so concerned about how they all felt, but a weight had been lifted off her shoulders. It seemed silly to be worrying about what these people, who she had only just met and didn't know, thought about her in the first place.

"Well, I hope the police looking into her apparent disappearance won't cause any more problems," she said brightly, feeling much more relaxed.

He looked at her sharply with a frown. "They still think it might be Jessie? But what about the postcards?"

Helena looked at him with surprise. She had forgotten he'd seized on the idea of Jessie sending the postcards as a reason why it couldn't have been Jessie. Although he had said people weren't upset about Jessie anymore, he certainly seemed put out the moment she suggested perhaps the police hadn't just let things go.

"Well, they're not convinced they came from Jessie. There were a few things about them that suggested anyone could have sent them. John wasn't sure it was even her writing," Helena said, wondering if she should be saying anything at all, given his reaction a few moments ago, added to the fact she didn't know what the police had discovered.

"Well, you have looked into this, haven't you," Bill said, staring at her intently.

Helena shifted uncomfortably in her chair, wishing she hadn't brought the subject up again. Would she never learn? The feeling passed quickly as Bill suddenly seemed to be back to his normal self.

"Listen, it's not the most comfortable of places to sit, here in this hall. Why don't you come back to mine for a coffee, and you can tell me all about what you've been able to find out?" Bill said, standing up and picking up his things. "I'd be interested to hear what you've uncovered, seeing as you seem to be in the know. It's not often we have a real-life mystery here on our doorstep."

He smiled at her as he spoke in a fatherly fashion. Helena was beginning to get whiplash from the speed his emotions seemed to change. He seemed irritated one second and friendly the next.

"Well, I don't know. I haven't got any other plans. If it won't put you out?" She wasn't thrilled at the idea of spending more time with Bill, but the last thing she wanted to do was upset him further.

She picked her phone up and sent off a quick text to David. *—I'll see you later. Going around to Bill's for a coffee.—*

Bill had been walking around the hall, turning off lights and putting away the small electric heater that had been next to the table. They made their way outside into the cold early afternoon. Already the sky had the wintery darkness that seems to arrive early, hours before dusk properly sets in.

"Come on. I'll drive us both around to yours," she said, standing with her keys in her hand ready to open her car door.

"Thanks." Bill walked around to the passenger side of the car and climbed in.

Chapter 19

The first thing Helena noticed entering Bill's house was how well-maintained it was. It should hardly be a surprise after seeing how neat it was outside. The difference between his and John's houses struck her. They were both men who had lived alone for a long time. They hadn't had a woman or anyone else, for that matter, in the house for at least thirty years, but the resemblance started and ended there. While John's house didn't look as though it had been touched since his sister left, Bill's house was surprisingly modern. With new furniture in the lounge, which had clearly been bought in the last few years. The whole décor of the house seemed fresh and brand new.

Although modern in style, it also lacked any personality or heart. There were no photos or personal effects on display. If she hadn't known it was someone's house, then she might have thought it to be little more than a show home or even a hotel. It wasn't what she expected from Bill somehow. Not that she had spent any time picturing where he lived, but she couldn't help thinking someone who spent so much time doing things for the community and working with various local groups might have had keepsakes and photos decorating his living space. There was something almost sterile about his living environment.

She looked around the living room. It would be

wrong to suggest it was uncomfortable as such, but the worn appearance of John's house had been so much more welcoming than this. While the actual temperature was warm, probably due to the heat pump humming on the wall above her, there was something cold about the room itself. It certainly showed no signs of Bill's wife having had any influence over the décor. It had been thirty years since she died, so perhaps that shouldn't be surprising. Still, Helena would have expected there to be some sign of her existence. A wedding photo or something like that perhaps. But maybe it was too painful for Bill to be constantly reminded of the wife he had lost and that was the reason behind the blank walls.

She looked through at the small garden area to the front. It was neat, well looked after, very much like the house. A few plants were growing, but much of it was given over to paving slabs and gravel. Almost as though nature did not dare to intrude into the well-ordered area. Those plants, which had managed to grow, were well-pruned and neatly kept in place. Many of them in pots rather than the neat borders.

"Coffee?" Bill asked, calling from the kitchen, just through the open doorway at one side of the room.

"Please," she said.

Helena continued to look around the room, taking in the light and airy space, while waiting for her drink to arrive. Before long, Bill came in and placed a mug on the small coffee table in the middle of the room. Helena had sat on the sofa facing the armchair where Bill now sat. She smiled at him and took a sip of the coffee. It was much stronger than she was used to, and she added a little extra sugar to counteract the bitter and overpowering taste. Obviously, Bill liked his coffee with an intense flavor. Not wanting to hurt his feelings by rejecting it, she sipped quickly at the burning hot liquid, hoping to disguise the taste with one of the biscuits he'd brought in and placed on the coffee table between them.

"Thanks," she said with a smile, looking at him. He seemed quiet and lost in thought and didn't respond immediately. She wondered if he regretted having invited her around and decided to drink up quickly and make her excuses to get back home as soon as she could to save them both from any awkwardness or embarrassment.

"So, you know about the postcards, then?" Bill asked, suddenly breaking the silence which had settled over the room. Helena looked up sharply, trying to decide how quickly she could make her excuses and go. The question seemed to have come from nowhere.

"Well, yes, John showed them to me. He just thought they came from Jessie, although they stopped a couple of years ago." She frowned.

"I take it then for some reason you don't think Jessie sent them?"

Helena couldn't help but feel a little flattered that she had maybe discovered the significance of the postcards and Jessie's signature on them. He leaned forward with an earnest expression on his face—perhaps he'd had similar thoughts himself in the past?

"No, well, I'm not sure, of course. You see, the signature never changed. It was always signed with a little heart above the I of Jessie. It just seemed to me unlikely a woman would continue to write her name in exactly the same way for all of those years. We all grow up and change over time and I just thought she'd have outgrown that as she got older."

Bill considered for a second. "Perhaps, but it could just be she never grew up, never changed?"

Helena felt a little put out since she considered herself quite astute to have noticed something as subtle as that. Bill seemed to be dismissing her ideas out of hand and didn't seem particularly impressed with them.

"Maybe. It just seemed odd to me, and John couldn't even be sure it was her handwriting. He couldn't remember ever seeing much she'd written before she left."

Bill nodded but didn't say anything else for a short time. Again, Helena felt uncomfortable. She sipped her coffee, trying to finish the last few mouthfuls so she could make her excuses and go. The room had begun to feel hot and close. All of a sudden, Helena wanted nothing more than to get out into the cool air outside and away from here. Shifting uncomfortably in her seat, something felt very wrong, but she couldn't quite put her finger on what it was.

"Of course, you felt the need to share these ideas with the police. You should have come and told me. I could have sorted it out," Bill said.

Helena frowned. "Sorted it out? I don't understand." She couldn't seem to quite grasp what he was getting at, and her brain felt sluggish as though she wasn't fully awake or with it. It didn't seem to matter to Bill.

He laughed but in a hard, humorless way. "No, you never do, you women." There was something in his voice now, a hard edge that chilled Helena. She decided it was time to go, but somehow, she couldn't seem to find the energy to get out of her seat and leave. She needed to…to stand up and…

"It's always a woman," Bill continued. "They ruin everything. I thought I had dealt with two of them thirty years ago and then another woman comes along and ruins everything like they always do. I lost everything due to that bitch." He spat the last word with venom and again Helena felt she should be doing something. Everything just seemed harder and further away.

Bill stood up now, pacing around the room as he spoke. She remained seated, feeling detached and distant, as if she was watching a scene unfold in front of her instead of actively participating in it. Unable to focus properly on what he was saying or doing or what she needed to do. It was like being trapped in a hazy dream, where she was merely a spectator and not a player in her own life.

"Jessie knew how I felt about her, she made me all of those promises. If I were single then she'd marry me, but I had a wife. Of course, everyone knew Pam had heart problems. They were all so sorry when she died, so sympathetic. Poor Bill, left all alone, but it was the answer to my prayers. I could be with Jessie, and we'd all be happy. Of course, it didn't matter the reason that Pam was dead was that I'd slowly swapped her heart medicine for sugar pills. She hadn't a clue why she was getting so weak, I kept telling her it was just a virus, nothing to worry about. Stupid cow. I should never have married her. She was poison, trying to control me. I hated her."

He paused and turned to face Helena suddenly, his face twisted with hatred and venom. He was raving now, all of his past crimes tumbling out as Helena sat there unable to move or answer him.

"You didn't know that, did you, with all your meddling and poking around. Thought you were so clever just because you stumbled across Jessie's body. Asking questions, stirring up things that were none of your business, you interfering bitch! Jessie wasn't the first I dispatched. I got rid of Pam by cutting out her medicine and then just when she seemed her weakest, I told her I was leaving. I knew she'd fly into a rage and her heart wouldn't take it. I waited until she was dead and then went into town. I got our next-door neighbor to come over and check on her. I'd phoned up and said I was worried I couldn't reach Pam on the phone."

Helena's mind was swirling. Bill's words were like elusive whispers, barely audible and impossible to grasp. She couldn't seem to grab hold of the meaning behind what he was saying. How was it possible that he had killed his own wife and Jessie? The thought seemed absurd and unfathomable.

"I called Jessie and asked to meet her. I'd recently bought another house to rent out, from her father of all people, and I told Jessie she could move in there and then we could be married in another six months. Once everyone had forgotten about Pam a bit, didn't want it to look like we were rushing things. I'd arranged to meet her at the house and show her around—that's where I told her we could finally be together."

There was a wild elated look on Bill's face, as though he were back there, telling the young woman he was infatuated with that his dream had come true and they could be together. Confident she would be as happy as he was at the news of his wife's death. Even in her confused and weakened state, Helena knew that it wouldn't have played out the way he had hoped. His face quickly darkened as he relived what had happened next.

"She laughed at me. She looked at me and said I was a stupid fool if I believed she'd ever had any intention of ever being with me. She'd only come around because she wanted some money. She was going to leave with that no-hoper from the garage she'd been hanging around with. Some crazy idea of going off to Australia or something. She mocked me, said she didn't believe I'd killed anyone; I was just a fantasist. She called me a pathetic, dirty old man and said I must be mad if I thought she'd ever been interested in me.

"I couldn't believe it at first. I begged her to think about what she was saying and that we could be together just as we'd been talking about. But it was all a lie. She'd been using me for money and gifts then laughing behind my back. She wasn't laughing behind my back now, but full in my face. She said she wouldn't be with me if I were the last man on the earth and I was old enough to know better, so I slapped her."

He looked down at Helena with disgust, as though she too had been laughing at him and making a fool of him. In his mind, all women were the same and deserved to be treated in the same way. He hated them, all of them.

"I'd always known women were not to be trusted. I'd let her convince me she was different, but she was just as evil as the rest of them, and she had to go. I put my hands around her neck and squeezed until she stopped struggling and the light went out in her eyes. She'd stopped laughing then."

He was standing looking down at his hands, as though he could see Jessie again held there as he brought her life to an end. There was a satisfied look in his eye, as though it had been his greatest triumph. "I buried her underneath the footings for the shed at the back of the house I'd bought. Her body must have fallen loose with all the rain and fallen down the slope onto Back Beach. That's how you found her.

"When I got back inside, I found her bag. The one she'd packed ready to go and meet that no-hoper from the garage. She'd left it by the door when she'd come in. I burned most of it. It was easy to make it look as though she'd left. She'd already taken everything from her room at home, clothes and everything, so everyone just believed she'd gone through with it and left."

Suddenly, almost dramatically, the emotion drained away again, and Bill seemed much as he always had. A harmless, aging older man, gentle and no threat. He moved over to where Helena was sitting, slumped in the seat, no energy left to sit upright. She knew she should move or do something, but for some reason, she simply couldn't. She looked at him trying to focus, but it was more than she could manage. He stood over her for a few minutes, watching her.

"I think it's time you left. I'm not going to be involved in any of this. John blamed me for Jessie leaving. He knew I'd been in love with her, and he was convinced I'd scared her off. He started spreading rumors I was interested in young girls and that's why Jessie had gone. For years I had to lie low, keep away from the charities and committees I ran. People didn't want their children involved with someone like that, even if there was no proof. Rumors stick for years. Now I've finally started to win back my rightful place in this town, and I will not lose it."

He came behind Helena and placed his hands under her armpits, hoisting her up. She struggled to keep her balance as he began to walk her to the door.

"I came to realize it was all his fault, of course. He was the one who made Jessie turn against me. He was too protective; thought I was no good for her. If only she'd said something to me, I could have put her mind at rest and then I wouldn't have had to get mad and kill her. She was young and foolish. Not like you—you're old enough to know better, Helena, my dear, and you must pay for your own mistakes." He grunted with effort as he moved her along.

By now, he had reached the front door and was peering out to see if there was anyone around. He leaned Helena against the wall as he got ready to move her outside. The street seemed to be fairly quiet, with no one around. The pathway to his driveway was obscured by the large macrocarpa hedge growing there and he was able to maneuver Helena into her car without being noticed if anyone happened to pass by.

He pushed her into the passenger seat and fastened her seat belt. Once she was secure, he walked around the front of the car and slipped into the driver's seat. Pulling out of the driveway, he headed down the street and around to Back Beach. There was nothing that Helena could do about it.

Chapter 20

Helena, still in a daze, was not fully aware of the situation or the danger she was in. Her head kept lolling forward. No matter how hard she tried to pull it back upright, it bounced around in time with the car moving over rough patches in the road. She struggled to hold on to her conscious thoughts, groaning, unable to make any coherent sounds.

"I can't have people connecting me to you," said Bill as he drove, probably more to himself than to Helena being in no fit state to respond. "When they come and ask, I'll say I left you at the hall. Of course, they may question why you've taken sleeping pills in the middle of the day. I'll tell them you'd been complaining of a headache and said you were heading home. There's no reason they won't assume you've mixed up paracetamol with sleeping tablets. I've slipped a bottle of each in your bag, so they find them when they come across your accident. It won't matter if your dear husband doesn't know anything about you taking sleeping pills. I know the lies and secrets that your type keeps. Women like you can be relied upon to be untrustworthy; I'm probably doing your husband a favor. There are some uses for you women after all." He finished with a grim smile, holding no pleasure or joy.

Bill had driven Helena's car around the Back

The Body at Back Beach

Beach Road, driving along the track that she had walked so many times. Past the port with its stacks of logs, on further around from the tar-sealed road onto the stone track leading around the coastline. He drove on past the boat sheds, which were fortunately quiet at this time of year, counting on not being spotted in Helena's car. There was no reason anyone should pay close attention to the car and remember who had been in it. He had continued around the track, passing first the place where she had found the body some weeks previously. He glanced up at the side of the cliff where the earth had fallen away, revealing Jessie after all these years. It seemed fitting to him that Helena should meet her end close to the same spot.

The track followed the edge of the land, with the water from the Otago harbor lapping against the edge. Because it followed the line of the coast closely, it twisted and turned as it went. After a bend, the road straightened out a little before it began climbing toward another sudden bend and a steep drop down to the sea on the left-hand side. While much of the track was almost at sea level when it was high tide, this part of the track always sat at least twenty meters above the sea and there was a sharp drop with little more than a few shrubs and bushes to break any fall before it reached the water.

Bill drove the car on a little further and then turned it around where the road was a little wider. He sat for a second to see if there was any sign of anyone passing by. It had begun to rain once more and there was no one out walking or driving—luck seemed to be on his side. He climbed out of the car, had one last quick look around, and then leaned back into the car and released

Helena's seatbelt. Her whole body immediately slumped forward. Her eyes had closed on the journey, and she appeared to be in a deep sleep. Although the driver's and passenger's seats were separate, there was no central console to separate them. Bill reached over and pulled Helena across into the driver's seat. It took him a few minutes, grunting and pulling, and by the time he'd moved her over to the driver's seat and sat her up in it, he was hot and sweating.

Still, no one had come along and interrupted them. This was his chance. He fastened her seatbelt, holding her once more in place in the seat.

"Goodnight, my dear, sleep well, won't you," he said.

The engine was still running, although the car was now stopped. He reached over and moved the car into Drive, and then leaned back in to disengage the emergency brake. He was glad she drove an automatic—it made what he had in mind much easier. In Helena's car, the emergency brake was a pedal on the floor to the left of the brake and accelerator pedals, rather than a hand brake lever. It was a little awkward, but he was able to release it and also give the accelerator a small nudge as he moved back away from the door. He jumped clear, slamming the door closed quickly. The car rolled forward, picking up speed as it headed toward the cliff edge.. Bill didn't stop to catch his breath. He was already shaking and struggling to breathe, but there was no time to hang around. He couldn't risk stopping to see what happened and the longer he stayed in the area, the more chance he would be caught or at least spotted by someone. The last thing he needed was to be seen where Helena met her end, as her car crashed over the cliff.

Had it been a different time of day, he considered he might have been able to clamber down the bank and walk back along the exposed foreshore. Unfortunately, it was high tide and there was no route he could take here. Not stopping to watch what happened to Helena, he hurried back down the road, making his way past the few houses that were built at this end of the road. He reached the point where the road was asphalted again and hurried on, taking the path that led to the back of the school. If anyone were going to spot him, he thought, it would be around here, but he could always claim to be out walking. With any luck, no one would discover Helena's accident for a little while and he would be well away from the area when the alarm was raised.

As he hurried along, he pulled the hood of his jacket up. The wintery weather had returned with a vengeance, and a fine misty rain was falling. Someone walking with a hood covering their head would be unlikely to be noticed as unusual enough to raise questions, and it might help to disguise his identity slightly. The weather also meant the chances of anyone being out and seeing him were greatly reduced. His jacket was nondescript enough to avoid recognition, and his slightly quicker-than-normal pace would just look like someone hurrying to get home out of the bad weather. Everything seemed for once to be on his side.

The entrance to the train tunnel running from this end of town to the entrance to the port at the other end was just in front of him. It cut under the streets above and was the quickest and most direct route to the port area. He glanced around quickly to make sure there was no sign of anyone paying attention to him. There were no trains currently in the area using the line either. He hurried, stumbling slightly toward the entrance, eager for its shelter from the pouring rain. It would be hard to explain what he was doing if he were seen walking toward the tunnel entrance. It ran along the back of the local supermarket, and there was no reason for a person to be walking along the train tracks unless they were up to no good. Fortunately, the fence and cutting were high, helping to hide him from sight. He still gasped with relief as he slipped into the dark tunnel entrance.

Hidden within the safety of the tunnel now, away from prying eyes, he took a moment to catch his breath. Although the tunnel was often in use, with small engines shunting containers from the port terminal through to Dunedin and back, he was fairly confident there would be plenty of notice of a train coming and could get out of the way. There was a crossing at each end of the tunnel, both fitted with flashing lights and bells that seemed to ring for a minute or so before a train arrived. The tunnel itself was narrow, with only a single track running through its length, but he was sure he would be able to reach the other end in time if a train were on its way. Even as tired as he now suddenly found himself.

He couldn't help smiling as he made his way through the tunnel. Oh, he might have been caught out by these evil women, who were all out to ruin his life, but he'd have the last laugh. He'd shown them all, just like a man should. Every time one of them had got in his way, he'd been able to act as the strong man he was and put them back in their place, out of his life for good.

His original plan had been to head straight for his own house, but he was almost at the tunnel mouth, and a new idea occurred to him. The tunnel opened out next to a pub standing right next to the local library. He would have to walk past both and then up the street by the town hall to get back to his place. The longer he spent walking around, the more chance there was of him being seen by someone, which he'd then have to explain if questions were asked. There was another option. There was a good chance if he went down the small alleyway running between the pub and the library, he might be able to make his way into the library through the rear fire exit. If he played it right, it would seem as though he had been there since leaving the meeting, giving him an alibi for the time of Helena's accident. Now he just needed to hope the fire door wasn't locked.

He slipped between the two buildings and made his way toward the fire exit. He stood for a few minutes to catch his breath and calm his heartbeat. If he were going to pull this off, he needed to appear relaxed. The door wasn't locked when he tried it. He slowly began to ease it open, listening carefully for movement on the other side.

There were several people already in the library, but no one seemed to have noticed him slipping in through the door and moving between the shelves. He quickly made his way to an area at the back of the library where there were tables for people using reference books or wanting to read the local newspapers. Glancing around to see if he had been spotted, he quickly slipped a small collection of books at random from the shelves and then set them out around him on the table, as though he'd been busy working for some time. Wasting no time to remove his jacket, he balled it up, stuffed it under the table, and engrossed himself in one of the books.

Although to anyone who might have been looking, he looked lost in the book in front of him. He was taking the time to steady his breathing and relax. He sat quietly, staring at the book, but in reality, assessed the area around him. After a while, when he saw someone walk near to where he was working, he made sure to look up and catch their eye with a smile. It was important for people to know he was here.

"Hi, Bill, didn't see you come in," said Hazel, one of the librarians. "You've got everything you need?"

He glanced down at the books spread around him and nodded.

"Yes, I came in a while ago. I didn't fancy going home just yet, and it's hardly the weather for being out and about, so I thought I'd do a bit of research." He smiled with an attempt at sincerity and hoped she would later recall the conversation well enough to remember his whereabouts but be unable to disagree with his time frame.

"Let me know if you want any help with anything," she said, heading back toward the counter at the center of the library.

He was glad she hadn't paid close attention to the books he was reading. There was no common theme between them; photography, sewing and cookery were all featured in the selection. Not ideal titles for creating an alibi, but women didn't notice the important things, so he didn't need to worry. He began to relax and wondered how long he needed to stay there to ensure he was covered.

The quiet in the library was shattered when suddenly the siren calling the local volunteer firefighters out sounded in the street outside. The fire station was a little further down the road and they were called out to both fire and medical emergencies, being first responders for the small town.

Bill couldn't help but feel a sense of satisfaction as he heard the call to action to go and assist Helena. It had surely been long enough since the crash through the barrier into the high tide beneath to remove his problems. She surely couldn't have survived that. It rid him of yet another woman out to ruin his life.

Chapter 21

The mobile phone on the table pinged with the irritating jingle that had seemed amusing months ago when he'd set it as his text message notification. David reached out and plucked the phone up, glancing away from the book he had been reading. Helena texted she was going around to see Bill for a coffee. He'd completely forgotten she wasn't at work today, but instead was attending a meeting over in Port Chalmers. He wasn't used to her being only part-time yet, so it simply hadn't occurred to him she should be back by now. He tapped a quick letter K followed by an X in reply and then went back to his book.

David was completely engrossed in the mathematics journal, which Helena, no doubt, would have suggested was perfect only if you were suffering from insomnia, oblivious to the amount of time that had passed. It was only when he came to the end of an article and reaching for his coffee, found it to be stone-cold that he gave any thought to how late it was. Helena should be back about now. Or was it more recently that she'd sent him the text? He wasn't overly concerned. =No doubt she'd popped in to see someone else or gone to the shops on the way home.

He was just settling down to read another article in the journal with a fresh cup of coffee when a phone rang. These days it was so rare for the landline to ring, rather than their mobile phones, that he considered leaving it for a minute. No doubt it was just someone trying to convince him there was something wrong with his computer, or he needed to switch his electricity supplier or some other similar scam. Then again, it might not be. He put the book down and walked over to the wall where the phone was.

"Hello?" he said into the receiver.

"Oh hello, I was looking for Helena. Helena Statham. Is she there?" came a male voice on the other end of the line.

"I'm sorry, she's out at the moment. Can I take a message or help at all?"

"Um, no, no, um, I don't think so. Or maybe." The voice on the other end seemed flustered. To David, it sounded as though the man was not used to talking on the phone, or at least he tried to avoid doing so whenever possible.

"I'm her husband, David. I can pass on a message for you?" David tried to sound helpful and hoped the impatience to get back to his reading wasn't too obvious.

"It's John Andrew's here, I live over at Pūrākaunui. I don't know if Helena has mentioned me to you?"

It took David a second to register who he was talking to.

"Oh. Yes. She said she'd been out to see you a few times and I know she's been talking to you about your sister? Jessie?" David wondered how much Helena had said to John, whether she'd shared her suspicions of the dead body possibly being Jessie. He decided now was perhaps not the time to mention this bit of information or what Helena had said about the police involvement either. He had been more concerned about Helena's involvement in this case and how dangerous being involved might be.

"Yes, I, ah, wasn't sure if she'd told people about that. About Jessie I mean. I know she's spoken to the police and, to be honest, I hadn't thought much of it until now. But they've been in touch and confirmed that it is her." John paused and David wondered what to say. I'm sorry for your loss didn't quite seem to cover the discovery your sister you thought was living in Australia, had been buried in a bank of earth for the past thirty years.

"I see. I'm sorry. It must be quite hard to deal with." David raked his fingers through his hair with annoyance. The inadequacy of his words seemed to mock him, and he wished Helena were here. She was so much better with words and dealing with people when things like this happened. Not that she had ever had anything quite like this to deal with, but she was certainly better when it came to bereavement and emotional things than he was.

"Yes, but, well, it's not so much that I was calling about. You see, I've been thinking about back then and I've remembered something I'd completely forgotten about. You see, if she had gone to Australia as I thought, then it wasn't important. But if someone killed her, then it could make all the difference."

David wasn't surprised John had come to Helena with thoughts of sharing information, rather than calling the police. She'd always had this air about her that invited confidence. It was one of the reasons she'd been so successful as a counselor for all these years.

"Ah, well, perhaps you'd better tell the police. I know Helena's been interested and asking questions, but they are the right people to deal with this." David knew Helena wouldn't be impressed he didn't get all of the information for her, but she could satisfy her morbid curiosity later and give John a call herself to find out more if she needed to.

"Yes, I will mention it to them. It's just I know she sometimes has meetings with Bill, and I thought it best to warn her, just in case."

"Bill?" David asked in a sharp voice, suddenly on alert. That's who Helena was with now. "What's Bill got to do with it?"

"That's the thing. I knew she was leading them all in a merry dance. All of those men. But Bill was the one who had it the worst. Probably because his wife was sick…she died just before Jessie left, you know?"

"Yes, but what were you warning her about Bill? She's gone around to his place for a coffee," David said urgently. John seemed to be taking a long time to get to the point and if there was some reason for concern, then the sooner he let Helena know, the better.

"Oh. No. There was some jewelry, a little chain with a cross, he gave Jessie. The day after she left, he came around to get it back and I told him she must have packed it and taken it with her, as there was no sign of any jewelry in her room. Well, a few days later, I saw him again and he was wearing it. Said he'd managed to catch her before she went and got it back. At the time, I just thought that's what had happened, but it can't have, can it? Not if she was dead by then?"

David was scrubbing at his hair with his free hand as he paced the kitchen. Absorbing John's words.

Where was Helena? Was she still with Bill? If this Bill was tied up in all of that, then Helena might be in some kind of danger. Was this something to worry about or had John got things confused? It all happened such a long time ago.

"He couldn't have just tracked her down before she was killed and got it back?" David said, a hint of desperation edging his words.

"Well, no, it was the day after she left, he came here. Unless she didn't die for a few days, and she came back from wherever she was. That doesn't seem very likely, does it? He couldn't have seen her before she went to Australia because she never went. There's something else too. He used to travel with his work, not all the time, but often enough to Australia for the yearly postcards we got. I know Helena thought someone else could have been sending them, and it occurred to me it might have been him."

"I need to go and find Helena," David said, abruptly putting the receiver back and hurrying to find his keys. He had warned Helena getting mixed up like this could backfire on her, but it still hadn't seemed all that likely, even to him. He'd been as interested as she had in playing detective and getting to the bottom of the mystery, like this was some book or television series. He rushed out of the house and sped off toward Port Chalmers in his car, not entirely sure of his destination.

As he drove, David tried to remember where Helena had said Bill lived. He wasn't sure if she'd even mentioned it, but either way, right now, he certainly couldn't recall anything. He had called Helena on his cell phone before leaving the house several times. There was no response, and after ringing a few times, it cut straight to her answering machine. David swore as he barrelled along the main road in Port Chalmers. There was no sign of her car, and he wasn't sure he would achieve much by just driving around trying to spot either the car or her.

With no firm plans in mind, he drove toward the port and Back Beach. Perhaps Helena had gone there after coffee with Bill. She often went for a walk when she needed to think or just to clear her head or relax a bit. He thought to himself about how they would both no doubt laugh later over his panic. There was no sign of her car as he headed up the road toward the highest point.

Just as he'd decided driving around Back Beach was pointless, he noticed movement ahead. There was Helena's car coming toward him.

It took a second for David to process the fact that all wasn't well. In the driver's seat, he could make out a figure that could possibly be Helena, slumped forward, clearly not in control of the vehicle. The car was moving slowly but gaining pace as it headed toward the barrier at the cliff edge. He didn't stop to think about what was happening or if this was the best way to deal with things, but he drove forward quickly and put his car in between the edge and Helena's car. There was a sickening crunch as the car plowed into the side of his.

Sitting breathing hard, he gave himself a second to recover. His car had stopped Helena's, but it teetered precariously on the edge of the road, uncertain if the fence would hold his car and stop it from tumbling to the sea below for long. It was only the angle he had hit the fence at that had saved him. If Helena's car had continued on its route to the edge, it would have surely gone over and into the swirling water below.

Her car had hit the driver's side with some force and had buckled the door. There was no way he could open it, even if her car hadn't been wedged against it. The passenger door was tight against the fence, and he wasn't sure he would have wanted to risk moving his weight to that side of the car in any case. He quickly scrambled between the seats and into the back of the car, where he was able to force the rear driver's side door open enough to squeeze out. It made a grinding sound as he forced his way through and ran to the driver's door of Helena's car.

"Helena, are you okay? Can you hear me?" he asked, pulling at the door.

She groaned slightly and shifted against the seatbelt, but otherwise seemed unaware of him or her surroundings. He quickly turned off the ignition and undid her seatbelt, pulling her toward him. The adrenalin coursing through his body made him operate on autopilot.

"Helena, speak to me. What happened? Are you hurt?"

He pushed her head back slightly and moved her hair out of the way to see her face. Her eyes were barely open and not taking in anything that was happening. She was breathing, which was something at least, and there was no obvious sign of injury or bleeding. As he started to maneuver her out of the car, she gave another groan and retched before vomiting all over the ground by the car.

"Oh, sweetheart, what's he done to you?" David said, trying to hold her while she purged her stomach. "I'm going to need to get some help."

He lifted her out of the car and laid her at the side of the road, putting her into the recovery position, and pulling off his jacket to cover her and keep her warm. He sat by her for a moment, rubbing her back and trying to reassure her he was there.

"I'm here, I'm here," he said over and over again as he tried to dial his phone and call for help. His hands were shaking badly, and it was a few minutes before he could manage to tap out the number and put the call through properly.

Chapter 22

Bill had been back home from the library for around an hour when a knock sounded at the door. He had been expecting someone to come and question him. Taking a deep breath to compose himself, he went to it with what he hoped was a slightly concerned but not unduly worried expression on his face. Anyone would surely wonder why police officers had visited them, but of course, he had nothing to fear, having done nothing. So, he needn't appear too worried. If they did suspect him of anything, they would surely be watching his behavior carefully.

"Can I help you?" he asked, opening the door to the two uniformed officers. He noticed a third man with them, in plain clothes.

"I think we had better come in, sir," said one of the officers, showing identification for himself and the other two men.

"Of course, of course, come in," Bill said, waving them into the lounge.

"Can I get you a drink? Tea, coffee, or something?" he asked as they settled themselves on his sofa and chairs. He only needed to keep his head while they were here, and he'd be fine.

"No, thank you. If you'd take a seat, please, sir," said the man not wearing a uniform. It was the first time he had spoken.

Bill sat down, still doing his best to seem interested but not unduly worried.

"I understand you saw Helena Statham earlier this afternoon?" one of the uniformed officers asked.

"Helena? Yes, yes, she was at our charity meeting earlier. I chatted to her there for a bit before I headed to the library." He smiled at them. "Why, is there a problem?"

"The library?" the man in plain clothes spoke again.

"Yes, I was doing some research for the local history group I'm a member of. Hazel, one of the librarians, helped me find some new books I hadn't seen before." Hoping this was a subtle way of making clear he'd been seen there. She hadn't helped him, but he was confident she would at least remember his being there and back up his alibi.

"So, you didn't invite Helena around after the meeting?" the plain-clothed officer asked. Bill assumed he must be a detective or senior police officer of some sort.

"Ah, no. We talked about it, but she had somewhere to be I think," Bill said.

"I see. Only she sent a text to her husband to let him know she would be going around to your house for a coffee."

Bill thought quickly, making sure the smile didn't slip from his face. He should have considered Helena might have shared her plans with her husband. It was easy to forget the way people these days seemed unable to do anything without first texting someone. They were so married to their mobile telephones.

"Oh, she was going to, but then she remembered

somewhere she needed to be. I can't remember where she said now..." He trailed off as though trying to recall what she said. "She might have needed to head home for something, I can't remember. She'd mentioned she had a bit of a headache...perhaps she was going to the pharmacy? We decided to leave the coffee for now, so I headed down to the library instead, as I said."

One of the uniformed policemen made a note in his pad. Bill sat in silence, waiting to see what else they would ask. He desperately wanted to make sure that Helena was indeed dead. She must be. The car had been heading right for the cliff edge as he ran away from it. There was no way she could have stopped it in the condition she was in. The siren for the local fire brigade had been at least ten minutes later, she surely couldn't have stood a chance.

"Do you always wear that pendant?" the detective suddenly said, gesturing to Bill's neck.

Bill's hand flew up to the cross hanging there. He fingered it for a second, wondering where this was going, but felt relieved that they didn't seem to have more questions about Helena at the moment. Not that he was altogether comfortable with answering their questions about the necklace he'd given to Jessie. He had feared it had been lost forever until he found it in her bag when burning her clothes, the day after she died.

"This, well, yes. It was my mother's," he said, bemusement evident in his voice.

"And it's the same one you gave to Jessie just before she went missing thirty years ago?"

"I...Jessie? I don't understand." Bill leaped to his feet, still clutching the cross at his neck. They knew, somehow, they knew. The uniformed officers both stood, and Bill realized the doorway to the kitchen and the one to the outside were blocked by them. "I thought this was about Helena crashing. Why are you asking me about Jessie?"

Panic filled Bill as the carefully constructed web of lies he had spent the last thirty years hiding behind crumbled to dust around him. He moved his head from side to side, like a caged animal as he blustered and railed against what was happening.

"Yes, Jessie. The young girl you were obsessed with and then killed when you realized, she was playing with you. That Jessie." The detective hadn't moved from the armchair he was sitting in, and he calmly watched as Bill loomed over him.

"Bitch. That bitch. She asked for it. Treating me like that. She deserved it all." Bill spat the words out with venom.

"I think you'll be coming with us, sir." the detective said, nodding toward one of the uniformed officers, who came forward to make the arrest. As he was led away to the waiting police car, the detective opened the front door wider, ushering in the scene of crime officers waiting to take the house apart to gather evidence.

****

Despite his distance from Port Chalmers, John had heard about everything that had happened to Helena. After his fraught phone call with Helena's husband, he had been worried about what had happened. He'd never trusted Billand while he disliked him, it had never occurred to him that he might be dangerous. He'd felt fearful when he'd heard that Helena was in danger and then guilty that she had been injured. It was clear Bill had been involved in Jessie's death all those years ago. Now, here was another woman he hadn't been able to protect.

Then there was what had happened to Jessie. All of those years where he'd let himself believe she was living somewhere else, safe and happy. He felt foolish now— he should have looked for her, should have tried to find out what had happened. It had been easier to pretend everything was fine. He'd been wrong. Sometimes, late at night, when he was completely alone, he could admit that part of him had always known. The idea she could have stayed away all this time just didn't make sense. Jessie was a lot of things, but her loyalty to her brother and her love for him had never really been in question.

A knock at the door brought him out of his thoughts. Before he even opened the door, he could see whoever stood on the other side was wearing a police uniform, their image distorted through the frosted glass.

"Mr Andrews?" the young policewoman said as he swung the door open.

"Yes, that's me, John Andrews, how can I help?"

"I'm Sarah Hanover from the Port Chalmers station. I was wondering if I could come in and talk with you." She paused for a moment. "It's about your sister Jessie."

John nodded and moved back, gesturing into the room behind him and then shutting the door behind Sarah as she entered.

"Can I get you a drink?" he asked. "Please, sit down," he added as Sarah stood awkwardly in the center of the room.

"No, I'm good, thank you," Sarah replied, sitting down. John came and sat opposite her in his usual armchair.

"You're aware the body we found was Jessie?" she said gently.

John nodded; he remained quiet, waiting for her to continue.

"We're not in a position to release her remains as yet, but we will be doing so shortly so you will be able to make funeral arrangements."

"Yes, I've already given permission for the funeral directors to organize it with you. They said they would be in touch once we could set a date." He shook his head slightly. "There's only me left now in terms of family and I don't think she'll have any friends who will want to come to a service, so it will just be a quiet burial."

Sarah gave him a small smile. "You might be surprised. I think there are a few people who knew her still around. If no one else, I'm sure Helena will want to attend if she's well enough by then."

John frowned, almost as though in pain. The guilt he'd been feeling returned with full force when he thought about what Helena had suffered. The policewoman was right though, from what he knew of Helena, she would be there to see his sister laid to rest finally.

"She's doing well; it was no one's fault what happened to her," Sarah quickly said, seeing John's reaction, "no one but Bill, that is."

"I know. I just can't help but feel I should have done more to protect Jessie from him and if I had done, then nothing would have happened to Helena either."

Sarah nodded with understanding.

"I'm here today because there are some things we found at Bill's house which belonged to Jessie. Or at least we believe they belong to Jessie." Sarah reached into the bag she was carrying and pulled out a folder. She shuffled through the pages inside while John waited.

"I was hoping you could look through these photos and see if you can identify any of them as having been Jessie's." Sarah passed the pictures to him.

John flicked through them, memories of the young girl that had been his lively younger sister coming back with each one. Bill had kept hold of a surprising number of things. Her handbag and wallet were there, along with her bank cards, driver's license and passport. There were also less personalized items such as her make-up and the hairbrush she'd carried with her. If he'd done more to find her, if he'd contacted the police and told them she was missing, then these were things that might have helped. They would have known she'd never used her bank account again, that she hadn't used her passport to leave the country. That she had never left at all. It was foolish to think about it now, he couldn't change the past. Still, the guilt of not having acted hung over him.

"Yes, these are all hers," he said sadly, handing them back.

"I'll need you to sign a brief statement to that effect," Sarah said, passing over another piece of paper and a pen. "The driving license and passport are enough on their own but it's good to have confirmation that these other items were hers too."

"I wouldn't have thought I'd be able to remember

all of these things, but in some ways, it seems like I only saw her with them yesterday," he admitted sadly, shaking his head.

Sarah gathered up the paperwork once John had signed it and returned it to her bag. She stayed silent for a moment as though trying to decide how to tell him something.

"You will be able to have all of these back eventually if you want them," she said. "There is something else I can give you now."

She reached into the bag and then paused again for a second before bringing it out. She looked at John as though she didn't quite know how to show it to him. Finally, she pulled out a small, blue, leather-bound book, Jessie's diary. She held it out to him.

"There's nothing in here that relates directly to the investigation, and we have enough other personal items to help to show Bill's involvement. We would normally keep the diary, but there are things in there that are personal to Jessie, and well, it should probably be with a family member."

She handed the book to him and for a moment he sat just holding it, looking at the familiar cover. He wasn't sure if he wanted to read what Jessie had written—the idea of looking at her personal thoughts and feelings seemed wrong. But holding her diary offered another connection to her again. He wasn't sure he needed it though. Her memory was enough.

"Thank you," he said, glancing at Sarah and smiling before his attention returned to the book in his hand.

****

Later, after Sarah had left, he finally got the chance

to sit and read through the diary. He opened it and ran his fingers over his sister's writing. There were a number of times he'd seen her sitting and scribbling in here and times when she had read things out to him. But he'd never read any of it, not one word. He took a moment and then turned to the first page.

"I hope you don't mind Jessie," he whispered. "I miss you."

Hours passed as he made his way through the little book. There were events he remembered and those he didn't. He found himself laughing and crying at the same time as he relived his sister's teenage years through her eyes. He flipped quickly past the pages where she talked about Murray and their relationship. These were things he didn't need to know and were none of his business. There was something else though, something he knew all about if he thought about it—his sister's relationship with their father.

He knew Dad had struggled to deal with Jessie, to show her he did love her. He also had known Jessie hated the way their father was so cold toward them. Was it surprising that she flirted with Bill and those other older men when her relationship with Dad was so difficult and fraught? He'd forgotten how hard she tried to make Dad love her and then when that didn't seem to work, she'd done everything she could to anger and upset him. Just to get some kind of reaction out of him. At the time, he had seen Jessie as being a difficult teen, barely any older himself. But now, reading her words as an adult and remembering how they had been, it seemed different. Her father's violent reaction had been the last thing a headstrong young woman needed.

He knew their dad had loved them both in his own

way, but he just had never been able to show them. Caring became anger and arguments and the more Jessie pushed, the more difficult things became. He didn't fully blame his father any more than he could blame his mother for dying young and leaving them without her influence or protection. He closed the diary. Reading it had made him feel closer to her for a while but left him feeling terribly sad.

Chapter 23

A few weeks had passed before Helena felt fully back to her old self. The sleeping pills Bill had slipped into her coffee, combined with the crash had left her feeling drained. Tired and with aches, pains, and bruises. Knowing how close she had come to becoming the latest victim of Bill was enough to set her back mentally for quite some time. She had given statement after statement to the police and had explained over and over again to concerned visitors in the hospital and later at home about what had happened that day. By now, she was thoroughly sick of telling the story. David had been wonderful, answering the telephone and deflecting as many people as he possibly could to keep her undisturbed, but there were still too many people asking her what had happened and wanting to know what the real story was.

It didn't matter how many times she recounted what had happened, it still didn't seem real. She could hardly believe the seemingly kind and gentle man who ran all of those fundraising groups could be a murderer. She'd always thought herself to be a good judge of character, but she would have never guessed he was capable of that kind of cruelty. Killing his wife, the young woman he'd fallen for, and then, years later, when about to be found out, trying to kill Helena herself.

"You sure you'll be okay if I go back to work today?" David asked as he walked back into the lounge where Helena was relaxing on the sofa.

"Yes, I'll be fine." She smiled at him. "To tell the truth, you're getting under my feet and driving me mad. It's time you went back."

He grinned at her. "A man could be hurt by that kind of talk. I'm glad you're sounding more like your old self. I'll see you later." He bent over and pressed a quick kiss to her lips before picking up his bag and jacket and heading out of the room.

"Less of the old, thank you!" she called to his back as he headed out to work.

She was glad David wasn't treating her with kid gloves. She knew how worried he had been, but the way he joked with her and teased her now showed her more than ever things were getting back to normal. It was one of the many joys of such a long and close relationship.

Helena stretched out on the sofa with a book in her hand, a romance. It was light reading, but she couldn't face a murder mystery or anything heavier right now. After going through her own murder mystery, she wasn't convinced she ever wanted to live another through the pages of fiction again.

It would also be a little while before she found herself walking around Back Beach as she used to. As for the charity committee, it didn't seem likely she would be getting involved in that or any other local group soon. Her career in local volunteer work may have been short-lived, but it was eventful enough to last a lifetime. She still wanted to be involved in the community, but perhaps some kind of small part-time job, or voluntary work at the local museum might be a bit safer.

Both Cathy and Diane had been around to see her after she had left the hospital. Helena was fairly sure their concern was only slightly eclipsed by their desire to know exactly what had happened and find out how Bill had been involved. David had valiantly deflected them, to begin with, but she'd eventually relented and told him to let them in. They had been part of the story as well, if just on the outskirts. Helena thought they deserved to know what had gone on.

Bill's actions had shocked Diane. She didn't seem convinced he could have done everything he had been accused of. She particularly struggled with the idea he had killed his wife to be with Jessie. She'd insisted more than once it must have been an accident or he had got caught up with the drama of Jessie's death and remembered it all wrong. Even with all the evidence Helena had told her; Diane still couldn't quite bring herself to think badly of the man she thought she had known for so long. Perhaps it wasn't just Cathy who had held a bit of a torch for him.

Cathy was less surprised by the events. She laid everything at Jessie's door. As far as she was concerned, the girl was poison, and had it not been for her, Bill would never have been corrupted as he had been. In her eyes, Jessie's behavior was as bad, if not worse, than Bill's. As for Cathy's husband, Frank, he seemed to have been elevated to some kind of sainthood when she spoke about him. Any suggestion he might have once flirted with Jessie or been good friends with Bill was quickly squashed. Helena had just smiled politely at this, hardly surprised at the sentiment and certainly not having the energy or inclination to argue with her.

Helena had also seen John a couple of times since she'd been at home. He still had a lot to work through and come to terms with himself. The first time she had seen him, he had been very apologetic about what had happened to Helena, as though it was in some way his fault.

Finally discovering that Jessie wasn't in Australia, living a happy life away from home, it was almost as though a weight had been lifted. Helena noticed he seemed to be happier and almost younger, and at peace finally.

He'd also bought around Jessie's diary for Helena to read.

"I don't want to keep it, after all of this time," he'd said, handing it to Helena, "but I think she'd have liked you to have it, seeing as it was you who realized what had happened to her. I think she would have liked you. Neither of you ever took any nonsense from anyone. It seems right you should have it."

Helena had flicked through the diary, reading bits and pieces. It was full of the hopes and dreams that all teenagers usually have. Plans for the future, and frustrations with the present. Helena thought she might read it properly one day, but at the moment it just made her feel incredibly sad. Potential that hadn't been fully lived, dreams that never had a chance of being realized, and a life that had been ended before it had had the chance to start.

She had read the very last sentence that Jessie had written in it, though. Jessie had been talking about getting away:

I have to leave here. No one ever seems to actually manage to go away from here. They all stay. Not me. I'm off, look for me in five years and you won't find me in this stupid town anymore.

Helena sighed. She'd been partly right, no one had found her. But then Jessie had never left. She'd been here all the time. She hadn't been able to leave the town. She'd never made it to Australia or fulfilled any of her dreams. For the last thirty years, she'd been in Port Chalmers, not going off to make her way in the world, just like all of the other local people she scorned.

A word about the author...

Kelly Jo Sweeney grew up in England before moving to New Zealand where she now lives with her Kiwi husband and four wonderful children. An avid reader from an early age, crime novels have long been a favourite. She always likes to work out whodunnit before the big reveal and writing her own novels means that there's at least one that she'll always got right. Her debut novel is set in and inspired by the unique scenery of New Zealand, infusing her stories with a wonderful sense of place and atmosphere.
www.kellyjosweeney.com

Thank you for purchasing
this publication of The Wild Rose Press, Inc.

For questions or more information
contact us at
info@thewildrosepress.com.

The Wild Rose Press, Inc.
www.thewildrosepress.com

Milton Keynes UK
Ingram Content Group UK Ltd.
UKHW021105200524
442968UK00015B/982